Girl Singer

Also by the author

Riding on Duke's Train
Travels With Louis

Girl Singer

MICK CARLON

Leapfrog Press
Fredonia, New York

Published in 2015 in the United States by
Leapfrog Press LLC
PO Box 505
Fredonia, NY 14063
www.leapfrogpress.com

Photos courtesy of Heinz Praeger

Printed in the United States of America

Distributed in the United States by
Consortium Book Sales and Distribution
St. Paul, Minnesota 55114
www.cbsd.com

First Edition

Library of Congress Cataloging-in-Publication Data

Carlon, Mick.
Girl singer / by Mick Carlon.
1 online resource.
Summary: "1938: eighteen-year-old Avery, aspiring singer, is heard by Lester "Pres" Young, Count Basie's tenor saxophonist. Pres recommends her to Basie, and Avery is whisked into the jazz life. Years later, with several hit records to her credit, Avery settles in Greenwich Village. But her life takes a sharp turn when she meets Karl, a Jewish refugee from Hitler's Germany"-- Provided by publisher.
Description based on print version record and CIP data provided by publisher; resource not viewed.
ISBN 978-1-935248-74-3 (epub) -- ISBN 978-1-935248-73-6 (paperback)
[1. Singers--Fiction. 2. Musicians--Fiction. 3. African Americans--Fiction. 4. Jazz--Fiction. 5. Coming of age--Fiction. 6. Holocaust survivors--Fiction. 7. Basie, Count, 1904-1984--Fiction.] I. Title.
PZ7.C216378
[Fic]--dc23
2015027297

For Heinz Praeger (1911-1997)
—a lion-hearted warrior of nonviolence.

Contents

One

A snowy Sunday morning in Harlem and I was trudging to work. I could almost hear the snores from behind all the brick and stone apartment buildings as I rounded West 145th Street onto 7th Avenue. My feet crunching in the fresh snow, I felt like I owned the silent city.

Big Joe's Diner smelled perfectly of coffee and bacon as I stepped in. *Ting!* An elderly couple, talking quietly in their booth, were the only customers. Duke Ellington's *Blue Light* was playing softly on the radio.

"Hey, for once she's not late," said Big Joe, flipping an omelet on the grill, a cigarette dangling from his lower lip.

"Good morning, Avery," said Mrs. Wing, the lovely Chinese lady who worked with me most mornings.

"There's a plate of eggs in the kitchen, still hot, waiting for you," said Big Joe.

"Thanks, Joe. Good morning, Mrs. Wing," I said, shrugging into my blue and white striped apron. "It's really snowing out there."

Joe gave the omelet another flip. "Nothing gets past you, girl."

In the kitchen, I was digging into those eggs—scrambled in bacon grease, hot and fluffy—for all I was worth. Joe's coffee was so strong I could almost hear the hairs sprouting on my chest.

"Did you sing last night?" Mrs. Wing asked.

"Yup—three songs. Hit every note. A rich-looking dude even gave me a fiver."

Working at the diner wasn't my only job. On Friday and Saturday nights I waitressed at a dive called the Hot-Cha, owned by a gangster who was never there. Some nights the four piece band—all pals of mine—allowed me to climb up on the rickety stage and sing a few songs for tips. I wasn't half dreadful. Anything to help pay the rent on my snug apartment on West 145th Street. For a 19-year-old who had ditched home eight months earlier, I wasn't doing too shabbily.

"What songs did you sing?" Mrs. Wing was my biggest fan. Some nights she and her husband would drop by to clap, whistle, and dance. They seemed like each other's dearest friend.

"Oh, *He Ain't Got Rhythm*, *Miss Brown to You*, and *He's Funny That Way*."

Mrs. Wing slapped her hands together. "Oh, I love when Billie sings those songs. I bet you sang them beautifully, too."

She meant Billie Holiday, one of our—and all of Harlem's—favorite singers. (Our other favorite was Ella Fitzgerald). I'd seen Billie once, stepping out of a cab, holding a tiny dog. I said *hello*, but I guess she didn't hear me.

"I was okay. Thanks, Mrs. Wing. You and Mr. Wing are my personal fan club."

Eggs eaten, it was time to work. The snow was still falling outside the diner's steamy windows and a few more customers had straggled in, ringing the tin bell above the door. I'd been working for about an hour when the bell rang again—*Ting!*—and a tall figure in a long black coat, his pork pie hat splattered with snow, ambled in. Looking rather lost, he sat himself down in a booth. No one in the half-empty diner noticed him—but I did. He was Lester Young, the great *Pres*, Count Basie's tenor saxophonist. Back in my tiny apartment, I owned a Victrola record player and a small collection of discs—we called them 78s: some Duke Ellington; some Louis Armstrong; a few Ella Fitzgerald with Chick Webb; some Count Basie (with his heavenly tenor duo, Pres and Herschel Evans); and my absolute favorites: Billie Holiday with her Pres. In exchange for Billie giving him the perfect nickname—the *President of the Tenor Sax*—Lester had returned the favor, dubbing her *Lady Day*.

Now here he was—*Pres!*—sitting in one of Mrs. Wing's booths, seemingly daydreaming, staring out at the falling snow. When I nudged the good lady and asked, she said, "Sure thing. He's all yours, sweetie."

Pres still wore his pork pie hat; melting snow was dripping onto his shoulders. He smelled of witch hazel and a fresh shave.

"Would you like some coffee, sir?" I asked.

Up close, his eyes looked baggy, lonely. He smiled a snaggle-toothed smile. "I'd have big eyes for that, startled doe."

Everyone in Harlem knew that Pres spoke his own language. It was said that even Count Basie had trouble understanding his star tenorman. Yet some of Pres' slang was catching on. People were beginning to call New York City the *Big Apple*, and now, if you thought something was *the cat's pajamas*—a 1920's term, so hopelessly out-of-date—you called it, simply, *hip*.

I knew that having *big eyes* for something meant that he liked it: "I have *big eyes* for those shoes," for example. Yet I wasn't to learn for a while that I'd been complimented: a *startled doe* meant a beautiful girl.

When I brought over the coffee pot and a mug, Pres had taken off his hat. I was startled by how long his reddish hair was in the back, almost reaching his shoulders. Pres was a lighter-skinned black man, with a few freckles across his nose. Being lighter-skinned, however, had not protected him from *feeling a draft*—in

Pres-speak, being confronted with prejudice. Pres had the saddest eyes, the loneliest eyes—eyes that seemed as though they had seen things that you hoped you would never see.

I couldn't help but notice that he was looking me up and down. Not to be stuck-up, but I *was* a pretty thing way back then, tall and slim.

"Weren't you singing last night at the Hot-Cha?" he asked. Although a large man, Pres had a light voice, high, almost whiny. I was so startled that I dropped a fork.

"You were there?" I asked.

Pres smiled his lazy, snaggle-toothed smile. "You dig who I am?"

Deciding to tease him, I said, "Yes, I love your playing, Mr. Evans."

For a second, Pres actually looked hurt that I'd confused him with his fellow tenorman, Herschel Evans. But then he must have seen my smile. "Ah, a *tricky* startled doe," he said.

"But I didn't see you."

"Hard to see with your eyes closed."

It was true. Although I briefly opened my eyes between songs, I usually sang with my eyes shut tight. Terror will do that.

Pres ordered up some bacon and eggs (and more coffee). Staring out the window, he seemed so lost, his eyes watching who knows what. Soon a rush of customers burst in, bringing the frosty air in with them, so I was busy for a while. When I looked up, Pres was gone. On his table, though, lay a five dollar tip and a slip of paper with a phone number on it. *Call me, S.D.*, it read.

"Mr. Young likes you, Avery," said Mrs. Wing.

"Mr. Young doesn't know me."

"Ah, but he likes what he sees. You should call him."

"Does he know how old she is?" called Joe from the kitchen.

Too bad I couldn't afford a phone in my apartment.

Two

I don't know why but I waited a few days before calling Pres' number. Shivering inside a phone booth that smelled of stale cigars, I was one cold girl.

"Hell-low," said a raspsy voice I'd know anywhere.

"Miss Holiday?" I asked.

"Who the hell wants to know?" snapped my idol, Lady Day.

"I'm sorry . . . um . . . my name is Avery—Avery Hall. Pres left me this number a few days back."

"Pres!" she called. "It's some bitch for you. Here he is," she said to me.

"Bells," said that high, slightly whining voice. I could only suppose that *Bells* translated in Pres-speak to *Hello*.

"Hello, Mr. Young. This is Avery Hall. I was your waitress at Big Joe's a few mornings back. It was snowing?"

"Oh, yeah . . . the singer. The Hot-Cha. Bells. . . ."

Stamping my feet to nab some feeling back into my toes, I was in no mood to listen to mumbo-jumbo. "I don't know what you mean by *bells,* but you left me your phone number."

I could hear Pres chuckling. "No harm meant, Startled Doe. Meet me at Big Joe's in an hour. Dress nicely." *Click.*

My rent included heat and electricity, but my landlord did

not supply me with clothes. I only owned three dresses: my red singing dress; a blue everyday number; and the green wool dress I was wearing at the moment. After washing my face and brushing my teeth, I figured I looked presentable enough, so I was waiting in a back booth a half hour later.

"Did Pres say why?" asked Big Joe, his ciggie doing a crazy dance over his lower lip.

"No. He just said to be here in an hour and to dress nicely."

"You look very nice, Avery," said Mrs. Wing. The diner was quiet, with only a few customers reading their *Daily News*. Strangely, Count Basie's *Blue and Sentimental* was playing on the radio. "I think he's sweet on you," she added with a girlish giggle.

Big Joe looked affronted. "Does he know how old you are? Pres is thirty at least. You're too young, girl."

Patting Big Joe's huge hand, I smiled. I'd never known my own father, so his paternal concern was appreciated.

Time inched along and my friends had to dive back into work. I'd almost given up on Pres when the bell above the diner door said *Ting!* and in strolled two men in dark overcoats: Pres and Count Basie!

"She's in the back booth, gents," said Big Joe, with a jerk of his thumb.

This is one of those important moments in a person's life, I thought to myself. I could see Count Basie—with his open, kind face—looking me over. *Please like what you see.*

Hanging up their coats, the two famous musicians sat down. Reaching over, Basie shook my hand. He had a kind smile, with wide spaced eyes that were not afraid to look into your own. I was hoping my hand wasn't damp.

"Pres said you were pretty—and he wasn't lying."

If I'd been a white girl, I would have turned scarlet. "Thank you, Mr. Basie."

"Please, simply call me *Basie*—or *Bill*."

Suddenly Mrs. Wing appeared, steaming coffee pot in hand. "Coffee, gentlemen?"

"Big eyes," murmured Pres. "Big eyes."

Basie chuckled. "That means *Yes*, ma'am."

"Anything to eat?" asked the good lady. "Food very good here."

"Not for me," said the famous bandleader. "Pres? Miss Hall?"

I shook my head, too terrified and wonderfully excited to eat.

Taking his first sip, Basie looked me in the eye. "Let's get to the point: Billie has skedaddled and I need a new singer. Pres says that you're very, very good—and I trust Pres."

"Smotherin' heights. . . ," said the saxophonist, staring out the window at a passing hearse.

"Starting when?" *This is really happening*, I thought.

"Tonight—then we're heading out on tour tomorrow."

"Well, I'd have to give Big Joe at least two weeks notice."

From the kitchen came Joe's booming voice: "No you don't, girl! You go with the Count!"

And so I did.

Mrs. Wing, however, had popped up out of nowhere with a stern look on her face. "How much you pay this girl?" she asked.

Count Basie smiled his sweetest smile. "Eighty dollars a week."

"Ew. That's good. More than here." The stern look reappeared. "She's a good girl, you know. Very pretty—but good. How you people travel?"

"By Blue Goose, our bus—and then we stay in various hotels or boarding houses in the towns and cities we play."

"Lady China," said Pres, "Lady Avery will be as precious as one's own baby sister."

Reaching into his jacket pocket, Basie pulled out a contract. "It's for six months," he explained. "At the end of six months, if you're not enjoying the ride, feel free to jump off the bus. And if we're not taken with your singing—"

"Ain't gonna happen," said Pres, staring out the window.

"Then we're free to say *Toodle-oo*."

Big Joe had been hovering. "Let me read that, girl." Grabbing the contract in his huge paws, the dear man read it slowly and twice. "It's fair, Avery. Nothing shifty at all." He looked at both Count and Pres. "It's good to know that men whose music I dig are also upfront businessmen."

"Like yourself, Lady Joe," murmured Pres. "Like yourself."

A bit taken aback at being called *Lady*, Big Joe kissed me on the forehead. "Now go home, pack up your rags, and sing your soul out, girl."

Three

My landlord said, "As long as I receive that check on the first of the month, I don't care where you go." Despite my excitement (and nerves), I was sad to be leaving my little apartment. After leaving my mother (and her latest boyfriend, who, like all the others, had fists) back in Yonkers, it was sheer heaven to have my *own* home, my *own* refuge.

After packing my three dresses, some slacks and shirts, a few pair of shoes, and my underthings in my secondhand trunk, I gathered a fistful of dimes and headed to my neighborhood phone booth, which today smelled of someone's tossed cookies.

"Mama?"

"Avery? What's wrong, baby?"

I could hear the boyfriend—his name was Ted—in the background. Our parting had not been pleasant, especially for Ted.

"Nothing, Mama. I have good news."

"Will you *shut up*? I'm trying to listen to my daughter!" I heard the sound of Ted slamming (luckily, only) a door—then silence. "I'm back. He's gone."

"If only for good," I said.

"I know, baby—but he has a good side, too. What's your news?"

I looked up at the gray sky; a light snow had just begun. "I'm going to be singing with Count Basie! Pres heard me singing at a club and then Count Basie walked into Big Joe's and. . . ." I told her the whole story, for once not having to embellish a thing.

"But where's Billie?" she said when I was through.

"She's quit." For the first time the thought struck me: *I am replacing Billie Holiday in the Count Basie Orchestra!*

I could hear that Mama was crying. "I'm proud of you, baby. Just you be careful on the road. Plenty of bad men out there, baby."

You should know, I thought to myself. Normally, I would have said it out loud, but I didn't want to spoil the moment.

"I love you, Mama."

"Love you, too, baby. I'm very proud of my Avery."

"'Bye, Mama."

"'Bye, baby."

Click.

A sudden idea: The snow was now falling thick and fast as I hustled past the cliffs by City College (whose stone buildings always reminded me of ancient Irish castles). Entering an apartment building on West 147th Street, I could hear the various cries and shouts of all the kids behind a green apartment door on the first floor. My friend Debbie answered.

"Look at you!" she said, smiling. "I *told* you to use a dandruff shampoo."

Debbie, who also worked at Big Joe's, was studying to be a nurse at City College. Yet studying in her family's apartment, crazy with kids, was always difficult. Usually she was nestled in a corner of the huge college library.

"Here, girl," I said, pressing a spare key in her palm. "I'm going on the road with Count Basie and my apartment is *yours*. Move in if you want—or just use it as a place to study. The heat is always pumping and there's always plenty of hot water."

"Hey, Mama!" she called, grabbing her coat. "I'm going over to Avery's for a while."

As we walked down the snow-muffled sidewalk, I told the tale of my good fortune. Deb hooked her arm in mine. "You know you're gonna be on a bus with a bunch of men, right?"

"I know that. I'm not stupid."

"Is there a toilet on that bus?"

This hadn't occurred to me. "Probably not."

"What happens when you have your ladies?"

This hadn't occurred to me either. "I guess I ask the bus driver to pull over to a rest room."

Debbie had a way of cutting to the bone. "What if you're not welcome in that rest room because you're black?"

I laughed. "Do you want my apartment or not?"

She kissed me on the cheek. "Just be careful, girl, that's all I'm saying. Be careful."

When we arrived at my apartment building, a cab was idling by the curb. The cabbie rolled down his window. "Hey, are you Avery Hall?" he asked.

"Yeah."

"Man, I've been ringing your bell for quite a spell. Count Basie asked me to help you with your trunk and get you to the Woodside. Something's up—not quite sure what. Let's get going, girl."

After the driver hauled out my trunk, I handed Debbie my apartment key and climbed into the cab.

I was on the road.

Four

Debbie was right: I was going to be the only woman on the bus. If you will bear with me, it would give me great pleasure to reminisce in words as I describe the members of the band:

Count Basie: *A kind man, a quiet man, Bill Basie could swing his band with just one finger. Jo Jones on drums, Walter Page on bass, Freddie Green on guitar, and Count's spare, swinging piano comprised the All-American Rhythm Section. When they were cooking—which was every moment of every night—that band hummed like the finest, smoothest engine in the world. Basie always treated me kindly, honestly.*

Buck: *Possibly the handsomest man in history, Buck had the sharp green eyes of a cat, and he played his trumpet with razor precision and buckets of soul. He had lived for several years in Shanghai, China, and could be quite mysterious. Buck played those city blues like they've never been played. The ladies swooned over his little-boy dimples—but Buck was no little boy.*

Papa Jo: *Always chomping on his beloved Wrigley's Spearmint gum, Jo is impossible to describe—but I'll try. Philosopher, philanthropist, teacher, talker extraordinaire, and the finest drummer in jazz, Papa*

Jo was one of the most fascinating souls I've ever known. The critic Nat Hentoff called him "the man who played like the wind," but Jo also thought, spoke, walked, and dreamed like the wind. His voice? Low, gravelly—like Popeye's—but Jo spoke with grace, proper diction, and with a wealth of reading and life experience behind his words. And his dimpled smile? Made the ladies swoon.

***Lester:** a gentle, strange poet, he was the musician who brought a relaxed, cool, behind-the-beat feel to jazz. Pres spoke softly and walked softly in soft crepe-soled shoes. He hurt no one ever—except, occasionally, himself.*

***Walter:** Big 'Un, the sweet giant of the bass. A quiet, shy man, Walter had led many of Basie's men in an earlier band called the Blue Devils. Everyone loved Big 'Un.*

***Freddie:** Basie's steady-as-she-goes rhythm guitar player. For some reason we were always shy around each other. I always liked Freddie, but never felt I knew him.*

***Herschel:** Hersch was my brother, as well as my protector. I will love him until the day I die.*

***Dickie:** Basie's star trombonist was also a fine cook—thanks to me. When I refused to cook for my band mates—because I can't!—Dickie bought a set of pots and pans and a hot plate. On the road, his room was the place to be, with his speciality, red beans and rice, always simmering to perfection.*

***Sweets:** His real name was* Harry, *but because of the gorgeous sound he coaxed from his trumpet, he was dubbed* Sweets *by Pres. Although he did not suffer fools, Sweets was a loyal and brave friend.*

Little Jimmy: Mr. 5 By 5—almost as wide as he was tall! Jimmy was a gregarious, friendly man and a consummate blues singer. Unlike many in the band, he was always faithful to the love of his life, his wife Janel. When I'm the slightest bit down, I put on the Basie recording Sent For You Yesterday *with Little Jimmy wailing, and my spirit is refreshed.*

As the cab left me off in front of the Woodside Hotel—at 141st Street and Seventh Avenue—I was surprised *not* to see Basie's bus, the Blue Goose, ready to depart in a cloud of diesel fumes.

"Lady Avery, you're *on*," said Pres, sprawled on a faded couch in the hotel's rather faded lobby.

"What do you mean?" I asked, stashing my trunk behind the couch.

Stretching like a cat, Pres tilted his porkpie hat at a rakish angle. "Lady Webb is hell's bells, so Lady Base is *on*—which means you, my sweet canary, are on, too—Savoy speaking, I mean."

Quickly, I translated Pres' words: "Chick Webb is ill so Count Basie's band is replacing Chick's band tonight at the Savoy Ballroom. *So you'll be singing tonight at the Savoy!*"

I didn't know whether to jump in jubilation or puke in panic. However, I didn't have time to decide because Basie swept by with Papa Jo right behind.

"Come on, girl," urged Jo. "You're roughly the same size as Lady Day, and she's sending one of her gowns over to the Savoy."

Escorting me by the arm, Basie hailed a cab and I found myself wedged between the pianist and drummer as we sped to Lenox Avenue.

"You'll be singing only two numbers tonight," said Basie. "Do you know *Swing Brother Swing* and *Them There Eyes*?"

Did I! I had only worn out the grooves of my 78 shellac discs of Billie Holiday singing both songs—with Papa Jo Jones on drums.

"Yes, sir," I said.

Frantically craning his head and searching every nook of the cab, Jo cackled. "Who walked in? Are you calling this dirty dog *sir*?"

For the moment I was laughing, not throwing up. Even the cabbie had to chuckle. Jo had that way about him.

Soon the cab was pulling up before the neon glow of the Savoy Ballroom, the so-called "Home of Happy Feet." I'd been several times—to hear Duke Ellington, Chick Webb and once, the Count Basie Orchestra with Billie Holiday singing. Never had I dreamed that one night *I'd* be appearing here.

Following my new friends down an alley beside the theater, I was shocked to see a none-too-happy-looking Lady Day, in slacks and a sweater, leaning against a sooty brick wall. She was tapping her foot and holding a white gown.

"So. . . ," she asked, looking me up and down with an acid eye, "is *this* the skinny bitch who's replacing me?"

I must have stuttered out something sad because immediately I was wrapped up in a fine-smelling hug. Lady Day chuckled. "Had you, didn't I? Simply ride that *bad* beat that Papa Jo lays down and you'll do fine, girl." Releasing me, she cursed. "Man, here I go messing up this gown. I have a bunch—too many, if you ask me—so this one is yours if it'll fit."

"Thank you so much," I said, taking the gown. "Miss Holiday, can I ask you a question?"

"It's Billie—shoot."

"Why are you leaving Basie?"

Lady Day looked up at the sky and laughed. "Well, it ain't the music and it ain't the musicians, that's for sure. It's that damn ass *road*. You'll find out. Besides, I found me a steady gig in a club down in the Village. It's called Café Society and I start next week. Now you watch your ass out on that road, girl. Your Basie brothers can't always be within reach."

Then with another curse and a smile, Lady Day was gone.

"The Lady knows how to make an impression," said Jo.

A few minutes later, in a dressing room smaller than my apartment's smallest closet, the gown fit perfectly, smelling of sweat and gardenias. Glancing at myself in the dim mirror, hearing the sounds of the Savoy crowd and Basie's musicians tuning up, I saw a frightened 19-year-old girl. I saw the girl who less than a year before had cracked her mother's boyfriend over the head with a heavy skillet, watching him fall to the floor. I saw the girl who learned in a short while how to juggle plates of eggs and waffles and cups of coffee without spilling a drop. I saw the girl who enjoyed singing for spare change at the Hot Cha with maybe ten people not paying attention.

I saw the girl who in a short while would be Count Basie's next girl singer.

Five

For the first few numbers I stood at the side of the stage, smelling the Savoy's musty red curtains, watching the dancers and the band. The Savoy had two stages facing each other across a massive dance floor—but tonight there was only one band in town, Count Basie's, and the people had come to **SWING**. As Jo loved to say, "This band can swing you into bad health." You could *feel* this band—Big 'Un's heartbeat bass lines; Buck and Sweets' piercing horns; Herschel and Pres' jousting tenors; Jo's masterful drumming; and Basie's subtle, swinging piano—in your throat and in your chest. I don't care if you had lost your feet in the Great War—those babies would *still* be moving. Think I'm lying? Go out and buy some 1930s Count Basie records, sit back down, and *listen*: *Every Tub; One O'Clock Jump; Doggin' Around; Jumpin' at the Woodside; Topsy; Blues in the Dark; Swinging the Blues; Boogie Woogie; Swinging at the Daisy Chain; Tickle-Toe; Easy Does It; Lester Leaps In; The Apple Jump; Pound Cake; Taxi War Dance* . . . and many others. If you marinate your ears in this swinging music, you'll be doing yourself a wonderful favor—but you *still* won't be hearing what this band sounded like in 1938 at the Savoy Ballroom.

Man! And how can I describe the dancers? In the entire Savoy, I could see only two souls not dancing their feet raw—twirling, swirling, jumping, jamming Lindy Hoppers on every inch of dance floor. And who could blame them? The All-American Rhythm Section—Basie on piano, "Big 'Un" on bass, Freddie on guitar, and Papa Jo on drums—purred like the greased engine of some magnificent ocean liner in open waters. And the *faces* of those dancers—damp with sweat, eyes closed tight, like people lost in a powerful church sermon. A certain spiritual power was at play when Count Basie's Orchestra was in full roar—that's all I can say.

The sheer swinging sweep of their sound nearly made me forget that any minute I'd be called out to sing. Nearly—but not quite. Basie had told me that he'd introduce me and that my first number was *Swing Brother Swing*. As song followed song, I became almost calm. It all felt like a dream—and a person's not nervous in a dream, right? But then I looked down and *right there*, in front of the bandstand, not dancing but certainly grooving, were Billie and . . . Ella Fitzgerald, my other favorite, the star singer of the Chick Webb Orchestra. Due to her boss's illness, Ella had the night off. She was dressed in a red-and-white-striped skirt and a white blouse, her hair pulled back like a little girl's, and she looked lovely—not glamorous like Lady Day, but simply lovely. Catching my eye, Ella sent me a supportive smile.

From the side of the stage, I had a close-up view of Lester Young: His head back, his eyes closed, his horn held sideways—daydreaming Pres, playing his feathery blues. It was beautiful.

Finally—but much too soon—Basie, sitting at his piano, began to speak: "Pres heard a young lady sing a few nights back and recommended her highly. Folks, I always dig Pres' advice, so please give a warm hello to Miss Avery Hall!"

Were my legs really working? Did my feet actually belong to me? I really don't recall if the crowd's applause was loud or luke warm. All I recall is holding onto that microphone, closing my eyes, listening to the band start the song, taking a deep breath and . . . singing.

"Deep rhythm can't deflate me.
Hot rhythm still elates me.
Can't help but swing it, boy.
Swing it, Brother, Swing.
Don't stop to diddle-daddle.
Stop this foolish prattle.
Come on, swing me, Gate.
Swing it, Brother, swing!"

I knew I was swinging the song—but I wanted to swing it *my* way, not Billie's, not Ella's. (Especially with those two ladies standing right beneath me!) When you admire a singer, it's terribly tough not to copy her, but I tried my very best to tell the song's story *my* way.

Before I knew it, Herschel Evans was pounding the song home with a vivid solo that had the dancers shouting for joy. I'm not sure if the applause was for me, or for Herschel, or for all of us, but with my eyes now open, I bathed in it for several perfect moments. Looking down, I saw that Ella was giving me a warm smile and the *okay* sign, while Billie was mouthing "*You magnificent bitch*" over and over. In Lady Day-speak, I believe that was a compliment.

From his piano bench, Basie shot me a wink as I skimmed off the stage. For the briefest moment I was sad, wishing my mother had seen my little moment of glory. But she was back in Yonkers, probably fighting with Ted. About half an hour later I was called out to sing my second song—which I nailed. Confidence is a beautiful thing.

"All right, folks—that was killer," said Basie after our fourth or fifth encore. "The Blue Goose leaves in two hours—three a.m. *sharp*! Say your goodbyes and let's hustle."

I felt a tap on my shoulder: It was Herschel, the tall, handsome (and married) tenor sax player. "Terrific, Avery—really swinging. Welcome aboard!"

Sidling over in his soft crepe shoes, Pres smiled his sly snaggle-toothed smile. "Quite tasty, Startled Doe, quite tasty."

I looked everywhere for Billie and Ella, but no luck. Still, Ella's smile and Billie's salty praise were enough. In my new gown, I wandered out into the streets. For a moment I'd forgotten it was winter.

"Avery!" It was Buck, the trumpeter. He was holding my coat. Lord, that man had dimples. "Here, baby," he said, wrapping it around my shoulders. "We don't want our new singer to catch a cold."

"Thanks, Buck."

"Where are you headed?" he asked.

A sudden idea hit me: "Taxi!" A yellow cab pulled to the curb. "See you in two hours!"

Soon I was knocking on my own apartment door. Inside the radio was playing softly. "Who is it?" asked Debbie.

"Mrs. Roosevelt—open up!"

"Fired already?" asked my friend, looking me up and down. Her nursing textbooks were spread out on the kitchen table.

"Make a cup of tea and after my shower I'll tell you."

After showering, I dressed in some raggedy slacks and a sweater that I had left behind, cleared away a few nursing textbooks, and sat down in the kitchen.

"So . . . what's the big secret? Did the bus crash?"

"No. . . ." And I told her.

"What?" Deb's big eyes grew even huger. "My best friend sang at the Savoy and didn't even tell me?"

"No time. I didn't even know I'd be singing until right before. And . . . while I was singing . . . Billie and Ella were right out in front, rooting me on."

Deb punched the table. "Go *on*! Now you're *lying* to your best friend."

The clock over the icebox read *2:05*. Reaching over, Debbie placed her hand on mine. "Your life has changed forever, girl. Hold on tight."

I could feel the tears. "It's crazy, right? I *think* I'm ready."

"Just be careful, Ave. You're on a bus filled with men—crazy musicians—and you're a virgin."

It was true. Despite what several of my mother's various boyfriends had attempted, I was. Ted had tried several times—hence the skillet. Through my mother, I'd seen what men were capable of, and I didn't want any of them touching me.

Because I'd never had a father, I'd created one who often gave me advice inside my head. (I knew it was crazy—but if I already knew it, was it truly crazy?) Right then Imaginary Father was saying, "Debbie is right, girl. Just watch your back—and your front, too."

"They seem like good guys," I said. "Pres is a little nutty with his *bells* talk, but they seem like gentlemen."

"You'll have some wild stories, that's for sure." Debbie stretched and stood up. "Come on, I need a break from studying. I'll walk you back."

Grabbing Lady Day's gown, I followed Deb down the stairs. The streets were quiet for a change, with icy stars blazing over Harlem. A few windows had lights shining, but most were dark. The air smelled clean and cold. Deb hooked her arm through mine. "Last week I was walking with a waitress—tonight I'm walking with a star."

"Don't jinx me. Basie could dump my ass."

"Not going to happen, girl." For a spell we were silent, both trying to avoid the icy spots on the sidewalk. "You're a good friend, Ave. I can't thank you enough for the apartment. Finally, a quiet place of my own to study."

"Just turn out the lights and lock up when you leave," I said.

"You know me—I always triple check."

We had reached the Woodside. Even in the early morning hours, with all its windows closed against the cold, music was *still* pouring out. The Blue Goose was running, shooting out plumes of diesel exhaust.

"Damn!" I said. "Where did I leave my trunk?"

"No worries," said a voice—Buck's—from the bus doorway. "Pres made sure it was safely tucked in for the night."

"Well, I guess this is it—again," said Deb. We embraced, I climbed aboard the Blue Goose—and my life changed forever.

Six

At first I could hear muffled conversations and soft laughter, but then I fell asleep, rocked off by the bus. Once again, I dreamt of Imaginary Father. Mama said my real father had tore off when I was a baby, but Imaginary Father stayed to watch me grow up. He was loving and trustworthy. In my dreams he looked like me—tall, slim, with clear dark-brown skin, and brown, wide-spaced (*Basie-esque*, come to think of it!) eyes. Imaginary Father was always patient, willing to listen to my little girl problems. He smiled often and smelled of bay rum. I never dreamt of any real person as often as I did of this handsome phantom.

When I awoke my watch said it was close to ten a.m. The sky was a raw dull gray. The bus smelled stale, filled with snores and soft voices. Outside the windows lay a landscape of slag heaps and crumbling shacks.

"Lovely, isn't it?" asked a deep voice. Across the aisle sat Herschel, the tenor saxophonist, rubbing sleep from his eyes. So we could talk quietly, he sat next to me. I don't know how he did it, but Hersh always smelled so *clean*—of Ivory soap with just a hint of some woodsy cologne.

"Where are we?" I asked. I could feel the layer of grease on my face and I badly needed to pee.

"Just crossed into West Virginia."

"Why?"

Raising an eyebrow, he grinned. "A gig—unless you feel like coal mining." My face must have mirrored my thoughts. "Let me guess, girlie. You figured we only played joints like the Savoy and cities like Boston and Philly, am I right?" I nodded. Herschel laughed softly. "Baby, we play *everywhere*—to anyone who will listen."

Within half an hour the Blue Goose had reached its destination: Bluefield, West Virginia. Basie, up front, stretched and yawned, gazing out the window. "I was stranded here once with Bennie Moten's band. Place sure hasn't improved much," he said to no one in particular.

The boss wasn't kidding. Yards were littered with rusted-out cars and trucks and the occasional bicycle. Buildings that were not made of sooty bricks were made of faded, sagging wood. Looking up and out of the bus windows, I felt claustrophobic with the large hills (or small mountains), stripped of trees, surrounding everything.

By now all the musicians were awake, but quiet. Pres was dabbing a cotton ball with some liquid from a small glass bottle, bathing his nose and forehead. "Witch hazel, Lady Avery," he said. "Cleans up the greasies right away. Give it a whirl."

"Maybe later," I said. "Where are we staying?"

"Mr. Wah's," said Basie. "Next left, Sam," he said to the driver, a quiet man with skin as black as midnight. I realized with a pang of guilt that I hadn't said *hello* to this gentleman when I'd boarded the bus.

Mr. Wah's was a two-story wooden house badly in need of paint. Yet smoke was going up the chimney and Mr. Wah, an elderly Chinese gentleman, greeted us with a smile. "Welcome, welcome, to Count Basie and his musicians. The hot water heater is working this morning and Mrs. Wah is cooking up breakfast."

Basie put his hand on my shoulder. "We always bunk up in these places, but obviously you'll have your own room. It might be small, but it will be yours."

"Thanks, Boss," I said.

The Count was correct. My dimly lit room made my tiny Harlem apartment seem like the Savoy—but it was spotlessly clean and warm. The bathroom was down the hall. I let a few of the guys use it first, then I took a warm bath, brushed my teeth, and changed into a clean pair of slacks and a sweater. I was now ready for Mrs. Wah's breakfast.

"Where are all the ladies?" asked Pres, digging into a pile of hot pancakes. Even inside, his porkpie hat stayed firmly on his head.

Mrs. Wah looked offended—as if Pres were inferring that her home was a cat house.

"He calls everyone *lady*," said Freddie, the guitarist. "Especially men."

Now looking perplexed, the good lady poured my coffee and hustled back to the kitchen. "Musicians," she muttered.

Soon all the "ladies" were assembled.

"So how do you like the road so far?" asked Walter, the bassist, whom everyone called *Big 'Un*. "Has its romance grabbed you yet?"

"Well, considering that back in Harlem I'd be the one pouring people's coffee, this isn't too bad," I said.

"You were excellent last night," said Sweets, the trumpeter.

"Really swinging, girl," said Dickie, the trombonist.

"Thanks, guys."

The dining room, too, was swinging—with forks and knives and spoons digging into all that good food. Mrs. Wah had cooked up a feast of eggs, bacon, sausage, toast, pancakes, and pot after pot of strong coffee. Soon our bellies were full and everyone sat back, satisfied.

"Has anyone taught you the whistle yet?" asked Jo.

I shook my head. "What whistle?"

Herschel, clearing his throat, whistled out nine melodic notes, then sang: "*I want you to get way back, babe.*"

For a moment I thought that maybe my breath stank. "Why?"

Jo laughed. "No, no, little Avery: *That*'s our call." He repeated the exact whistle, then chanted: "*I want you to get way back, babe.*"

"That's it?" I asked, trying to suppress a giggle.

"On the count of three, fellas," said Basie. "One, two, *three!*" The entire band whistled the tune, then chanted, "*I want you to get way back, babe!*" Mr. and Mrs. Wah poked their heads in the room to make sure everything was all right.

"Now you try it," said Dickie.

So I did. And I was in.

"If you ever get your fine behind in any kind of trouble," said Little Jimmy, buttering yet another stack of pancakes, "just give a whistle and a call, and your Basie brothers will have your back."

By the time breakfast was finished, it was a little past noon. The guys all trudged up the stairs to bathe and nap. "Let's be at the town hall by seven o'clock, gentlemen," said Basie. "Rest up."

"Oh, Avery," said Big 'Un. "Do you sew?"

"Um . . . yeah, a little," I said. "Usually I let a pro do it."

"A button came off my white tuxedo shirt last night. Would you mind?"

The idea rubbed me the wrong way. "No, I don't think so. Sorry. You can probably do a better job yourself."

Big 'Un looked shocked. "But Billie used to sew for us—and cook, too."

"Man, you don't want to eat my cooking! Can't I just be one of the guys?"

Behind the bassist's back, Pres was giving me the *okay* sign. "I have big eyes for this," he murmured. "Lady Avery has some nerve."

For some reason, Dickie looked happy at the news that I couldn't cook.

"Man, that's cold. . . ," said Big 'Un under his breath.

After drifting off for a spell in my room, I woke up around two. The second floor was filled with the sounds of snoring. Putting on my coat, I crept downstairs. Mr. and Mrs. Wah were nowhere in sight. Quietly, I opened the front door and walked out into a chilly, damp, gray-sky afternoon.

A few people were out shopping on Main Street. They were mostly white folks, but I did see a few black people. All the men wore blue jean overalls and had a hard, beaten look on their faces. No one paid me much mind. I passed a bank, a barbershop, a library, a diner, a green grocer's, a butcher's shop, and a Woolworth's. In the five-and-dime I bought some toothpaste from a brown-skinned girl about my own age.

"Are you with Count Basie?" she asked.

"How'd you know?"

"Well, the Basie band is playing in the town hall tonight and you don't look familiar—*and* you're dressed better than anyone here." No one else was in line. "What's it like?"

"What?"

"Traveling with a band."

I laughed. "I've just begun. Two days ago I was waiting tables in Harlem."

The girl pointed to the clock on the wall. "I'm off in five minutes. Want to wait?"

I did. Her name was Betsy and in a few minutes we were

trudging up a hill. "We don't have electricity," she explained, "but we *do* have a wind-up Victrola and a couple of Basie records. But you aren't on them, right?"

"Not yet," I said.

The family's little shack was painted bright blue. An old Model T (with no tires) on cinderblocks stood in the front lawn, which was littered with various bones and children's toys. Two huge dogs explained the bones.

Inside the living area, which mingled with the kitchen (and I'm not criticizing: It was about the size of my apartment back home), sat Betsy's mom, who was humming and sewing. Behind a door came some mighty powerful snoring. A wood-burning stove was doing its job.

"Mama, this is Avery. She's Count Basie's new singer."

Betsy's mom was as pretty as her daughter, but she looked exhausted, as if constant worry was wearing her down. "You don't say," she said, revealing a gap-toothed smile. "Now how did this happen?"

As I explained my trip to Woolworth's for the toothpaste, Betsy put the kettle on a massive, wood-burning stove. Soon we were all seated, sipping tea. Betsy, winding up the Victrola, blasted Basie's 78 *Boogie Woogie*, with Little Jimmy singing. When the song ended, her mother simply lifted the needle, cranked the machine, and Jimmy once again swang the blues.

"You can be sure we're going tonight," said Betsy's mom, whose name was Betsy. "On Sunday my husband sleeps all day—he mines coal the rest of the week—but he's waking up soon, taking a bath, and we'll be there. Betsy, are you going to show her?"

"Show me what?" I asked.

"Something special," said Betsy, "but you can't tell anyone."

"Okay," I said. *Should I be nervous?* I thought. "I just have to be at the Town Hall by seven."

"No problem. Mama, where's the flashlight?"

"Probably where you put it," said her mom, rolling her eyes. "What's Jimmy Rushing like?" she asked me.

"To tell you the truth, ma'am, I don't know him that well yet. But he's been friendly to me—they all have been."

The good lady lit a cigarette. "Yeah, I bet."

Betsy was out the door like a cat, so I had to rush to catch up. She was holding a flashlight. "Where are we going?" I asked.

"My favorite place in the whole world. Wait 'til you see it."

Late afternoon shadows were creeping in, with the clouds in the west all purplish and frosty looking. We were heading up a hill, bare at the bottom, which became a rather thick grove of trees the higher we climbed. The air smelled smoky and I could see the main street of Bluefield far below, looking like the main drag of a matchstick town. Panting, I struggled to keep up with Betsy, who seemed to be half mountain goat. Finally we stood by a fairly large stone, me panting like crazy, Betsy barely winded.

"A rock?" I said. "You brought me up here to see a *rock*?"

That West Virginia gal had one sly smile. For a second I was sure she'd brought me up here to bash my brains out with the flashlight—or the rock. Instead, she fell to her knees and rolled the stone away. At first I didn't see anything, but then Betsy cleared away some yellowed grass and I saw it: a black hole going down, down, *down*.

Sitting, she popped both her feet into the hole. "Come on, let's go."

"You crazy? You expect me to go down *there*?"

Betsy was quickly disappearing. "It's not steep—and the ground is rock hard, so we won't get dirty." She was gone. "Come on!"

So I did. The hole did not plunge straight down, but at an angle, like a ramp. My eyes were shut tight the whole time. As I gently slid down, the air grew warmer, smelling of dirt, which is really not a bad smell, if you've ever noticed. Two hands grabbed mine and I was pulled to my feet.

"We're here!" said Betsy, flicking on the flashlight.

But where was *here*?

Up above, in a small circle, flowed the gray winter sky—but everywhere else was stone—stone floor, stone walls, stone ceiling. I could hear water dripping. Strange, but it was warm underground. Even though I kept it on, I no longer needed my coat.

"Follow me!"

"Let's not go too far in," I said. "I have a show to do in a few hours."

"Just a few steps," said Betsy. Every step that took us further away from that bit of sky seemed terribly wrong. We only walked for about two minutes, but it seemed far longer. Finally, she stopped, a triumphant smile on her face. "Close your eyes," she said. "Okay . . . now *open them!*"

I think I gasped. It was beyond beautiful. Betsy was shining the light on an entire wall covered in paintings—red, blue, yellow, green—paintings of deer and bears and fish and eagles and people. The people were dark-skinned, with intense eyes. Their bodies were slim and muscled. In some scenes the people, both men and women, held spears, obviously hunting. In others, families with children were seated around fires. The children were beautiful. It was all beyond beautiful.

"Did you do this?" I asked—for a moment doubting the sanity of someone who would paint underground.

"God, no—I found it like this. Daddy says it was done by Indians a long time ago."

My eyes were drinking in every detail. I now felt a bit sad, knowing that the artist and all of her (or his) models were long, long gone from the world. I saw a little child—tough to say whether a boy or a girl—fishing in a creek with a baby deer creeping up behind. Suddenly—blackness. "Oh, shoot—the batteries must have died," said Betsy. My eyes were open but it was like they were shut. *Are we trapped in here forever?* I thought in a moment of terror. Yet within ten seconds my eyes had begun to adjust and I could see Betsy, shaking the flashlight. A few seconds more and I could see the light from the hole in the distance.

"Have you told anyone about this?" I asked.

"No, Daddy says to keep it quiet for now. He says that if we tell the right people we could make some money for the discovery. I'd love to go to West Virginia State to be a teacher. Maybe the college will be interested in these and give me a free education." She touched my hand. "Please don't tell anyone, Avery." For a moment she looked as if she'd made a mistake.

"Who am I going to tell? And tomorrow morning I'll be gone."

"Well, let's go home," said Betsy. "I just thought you'd enjoy this."

"I did. And my best friend back home, Debbie, she's studying to be a nurse, so don't give up on that dream."

We were quiet as we climbed out and walked down the hill to Betsy's shack. Her father was still snoring and I said my goodbyes to her mother. "We'll see you at the show, dear," she said, kissing me on the cheek.

You know, I'm far from perfect, but I always keep my word—and I kept my word to Betsy. I never told a soul about those underground paintings—until now. I sure hope she was able to go to college and become a teacher.

Back at the Wahs' boarding house, I treated myself to a second bath. I could hear Pres' voice from the hallway. "We have a very clean startled doe on our hands, ladies. Better grab the bathroom when you can."

Seven

That evening's show at the Bluefield Town Hall was spectacular. Chairs were set up on either side of a center aisle, with the local white folks sitting to the right and the black folks on the left. Everyone seemed to get along—hardworking people out for a good time.

This was the night when I really began to see and hear what the Count Basie Orchestra was all about—soul, heart, rhythm and *swing*. One of Mama's good-guy boyfriends—the exception, I'm sorry to say—once brought me to a Memorial Day parade in Yonkers. I must've been around seven or eight years old and boy, could I *feel* those drums, those bugles in my throat, in my chest. I'd never forgotten that feeling—and the Basie band brought it all roaring back. People could *feel* that band! You could see it in their faces, in the way they danced, in their shouts of joy. Count Basie's band brought happiness to people—and it all began with that rhythm section: Count on piano; Freddie on guitar; Big 'Un on his beautiful mahogany bass; and Papa Jo, a wizard of artistry, at his drums. That rhythm section had a beat as *smooth* and *steady* and *strong* as an Olympian's heart.

This was the night when I also really paid attention to the band's two tenor stars, Herschel and Pres. Sitting at opposite sides of the stage, they never looked at each other. If you didn't know any better, you'd think they were enemies—but you'd be wrong. They loved each other as brothers—but man, they were rivals, too. When Herschel stood to solo, his sound was so deep, so powerful, that you could *hear* the heat of his Texas childhood in every note. With his face drenched in sweat and his neck veins bulging, Hersh's solo that night on *Topsy* was frantic, beyond intense. When he removed the horn from his lips and sat down, his fans screamed his name. But then Pres' fans screamed *his* name when he stood . . . slowly . . . slyly . . . to solo. Pres held his horn at an odd angle—tilted away from his body—and his sound was as different from Herschel's as a soufflé is from a steak. Lester's sound was lighter, airier, but no less rhythmic than his friend's. His solo that night on *Every Tub* brought the crowd to near pandemonium—and he didn't even break a sweat. With his eyes closed, Pres created new melodies every night—no solo was ever the same. Herschel was a rip-roaring dancer on his horn—but Pres was a poet. If Hersh's solos flowed straight from his beautiful heart, Pres' flowed from a corner of his dream-garden mind that was hidden from view—except in his music. After his solo, eycs still closed, Pres nodded to his followers, then slowly, slyly sat down.

Buck's trumpet was always crackling with energy, but never to the point of pain. Buck loved the middle range of his horn and played with precision and power. Sweets was more subtle—if three perfect notes could take the place of eight, then Sweets was your man. Years later he would be Frank Sinatra's favorite trumpet player. Both men knew their blues and played it every night for the people.

Speaking of the blues, no one *ever* sang it like Little Jimmy. I can still hear the way he'd turn *Goin' To Chicago* into such a joyous lament of pain that some ladies would cry out as if they were in church. A very fat man, he could also dance and skip across the stage like a black Nijinsky. I still wonder why Basie needed me when he had Mr. Five By Five in his band.

Speaking of Basie, he played his piano like a wise old painter. Let me explain: I love to read biographies and for a spell I ripped through books about the painters Claude Monet and Pierre August Renoir. As they aged, they began to realize (artistically) that *less is more*—that it's better to have ten perfect brush strokes than thirty mediocre ones. That, exactly, was Basie's piano style: He could drive a band with just three notes—but they were the *only* three notes. The Boss was beautiful.

And that was Freddie's guitar style as well. The band lived above his foundation of expertly placed, humming chords—yet unless you paid attention, you barely noticed. (Except on the rare night when Freddie was sick: *then* you noticed. The house's foundation had been ripped clean away).

I always loved Dickie's trombone sound—driving, roaring, with a sense of cool that only urban jazzmen possess.

And sitting up on his riser, magisterial, smiling like a benign king, chewing his Wrigley's Spearmint, was Papa Jo, perhaps the greatest jazz drummer of them all. (From a girl's perspective, I found Jo and Herschel to be the handsomest of the Basieites). Jo, too, was an innovator: transferring the pulse of the music from the thundering bass drum to the cool, sizzling ride cymbal. Simply put, Jo was a supreme artist, smiling down on his *kiddies*—the young musicians, fans, or *anyone* who wanted to learn about jazz. "This music is as serious as life," he said to me several times, "and if you want to learn it, be ready for a lifetime of study." Sometimes on late bus rides, my eyes heavy, I would wish that Jo would stop talking, but I have to admit that he was a fine teacher, of music and of life.

And when the band put it all together, *man*, you should have *seen* those crowds! Dancing, shouting, jumping, beseeching—people being baptized in the blues and loving every second of the night. No matter how wretched their day jobs, they were dancing and loving life. Count Basie's band was a traveling swing factory that brought nothing but joy to the land.

I was so caught up in the show that I had no time to be nervous. When I held on to that microphone and sang *Between the Devil and the Deep Blue Sea*, I felt exhilarated and absolutely free—like I was born to sing in front of this band. Looking out, I saw Betsy and her folks—her dad was a painfully thin man—swaying and looking up at me. Betsy (The Younger) smiled up and I smiled right back.

You know, I feel sorry for the billions of folks who never had the chance to sing in front of the Count Basie Orchestra. Have you ever noticed that with practice comes confidence, and with confidence comes true skill, which only increases one's confidence? This is what happened to me—with each song I sang, backed by that gloriously swinging band, I improved and improved. My versions that night of *Swing Brother Swing* and *They Can't Take That Away From Me* were miles beyond my Savoy performances. Now I would *never* compare myself with Billie and Ella—they were once in a century talents—but like them I found myself improvising, never singing the same song the same way twice.

I had found true happiness, and a true family, in the Basie band.

That night on the bus, changed back into slacks and a sweater, I was bursting to tell someone about the underground cave paintings, but I kept my word to Betsy. I've never heard of underground paintings being discovered in West Virginia, so I sometimes wonder what became of her. I hope nothing but good.

Sam, quiet as always, drove the Blue Goose through the midnight roads, passing shadowy fields and darkened shacks. Every now and again I'd see an all-night filling station with a *Coca Cola* sign lit up in the window. I was so jazzed from the show that I found it hard to sleep. At first some of the men, led by Basie himself, took part in a spirited game of dice in the back of the bus. But one by one, exhausted, the musicians all fell off to sleep. I thought I was the only one (apart from the faithful Sam) awake until Herschel, stretched out on the seat across from me, opened his eyes. Even from across the aisle, I could smell that fancy cologne mingled with Ivory soap.

"Do you have a boyfriend?" he asked.

"No—and I don't want one either," I said, not meaning to sound quite so salty.

"Hey, girlie, I'm married," he said with a smile, pointing to his ring finger. "But Freddie's desperate, so watch out."

"Man, I heard that!" called a soft voice from the back of the bus.

"And Big 'Un would crush you," said Herschel.

"Heard that, Hersh!"

Herschel had one evil grin. "You were meant to, Walter. Lay off that bacon, man!"

"Ladies, ladies," called that slightly whining voice. "Poor Pres is trying to dream of better times and no gray boys or Bob Crosbys." I could see the shadow of a pork pie hat several rows up.

"What the hell does that mean?" I whispered.

Herschel laughed softly. "A *gray boy* is a bigot and a *Bob Crosby* is a corrupt cop out to bust Pres."

"Those damn Bob Crosbys, out to bust poor Pres," murmured Lester as he fell back to sleep.

"You've been singing mighty fine, girl," said Herschel, leaning his head against the window. "What's your story?"

"Not much to tell," I said. "I was a waitress until a few days ago."

"How old are you?"

"Nineteen."

"You look younger. Now Pres heard you singing at the Hot-Cha. Right?" I nodded. "Yeah, Billie left us high and dry. Pres said you'd be perfect." A pause. "He was right."

"Thank you."

"Hey, it's the truth. And you're with a good bunch here. As a young lady, you have nothing to fear. We're pretty much gentlemen. But we're heading further south on this tour, so don't wander too far from us."

"I won't," I lied.

"Any family?"

"Just my mother in Yonkers. You?"

"My wife and little girl are back in Harlem. My folks live in Denton, Texas. It's a little town halfway between Dallas and Fort Worth. We're playing there at North Texas State next week. Can't wait to see them."

And that's all Herschel said. Soon we were both asleep, as steady Sam drove on through the 1938 night.

Eight

"Is our Avery a virgin?" asked Buck as our bus rolled through the snow-flecked fields of Kentucky.

"Excuse me?" I asked, feeling my face grow hot. "What the hell kind of question is that?"

"A good one," said Dickie.

If I'd been born an Irish lass, I would've been blushing like a July sunset. "For your information, I am. What is it to you?"

"Pay them no mind, Ave," said Basie. "It's like you're their little sis."

"Would you ask your little sister a question like that?" I asked.

"Yup," said Jimmy, grinning, "and I have." He paused. "Her answer was *no*, in case you're wondering."

The entire bus, even Sam, even me, cracked up. Sweets began the "Basie Whistle"—*I want you to get way back, babe*—and soon the Blue Goose was filled with that nine-note tune.

"Remember that," said Buck. "You're one of *us* now and we'll always be there for you, Ave."

Our next town was Lexington, Kentucky. After I lay down my trunk in our latest boarding house, my first task was cleaning my clothes. After the chill of West Virginia, the day felt spring-like, with the sun trying to peek out from behind the clouds. The neighborhood for black folks was mostly two- or three-story brick buildings, with sidewalks and plenty of trees. I found a dry cleaner who said she could clean Billie's gown in three hours.

Although I had to venture into a white neighborhood for the laundromat, I sensed no hostility, so I walked in. Picking up a *Life* magazine from a bench, I sat guard over my clothes while they tumbled. Time passed with no trouble—but then:

"Hey, look, LeRoy," said a loud voice, "a nigger who can read." A greasy, pimply white boy grabbed my magazine and flung it to the floor. LeRoy, even greasier than his pal, snickered.

A grandmotherly white lady clucked her tongue. "You boys should be ashamed of yourselves, bothering a young lady." I could have hugged her.

"Shut up, you old nigger lover," said LeRoy.

For some reason, I did not feel afraid, which shows how stupid I was. "Thank you, ma'am," I said, "but fools like these two have no respect for anyone—including their useless selves."

True words—but they earned me a stinging slap across the face. I was ready to dig my fingernails into the closest greasy face when—*sha-zam!*—there stood Little Jimmy, all three hundred pounds of him. Spreading his arms wide—*boink!*—he smashed the two crackers' heads together, just like Moe in *The Three Stooges*. Senseless, they fell to the floor and stayed there.

"Where did you come from?" I asked.

"Other side of the laundromat—I sit low-down." Jimmy looked worried. "I don't care if your clothes are still damp, girl—just grab 'em and follow me."

Tipping his hat to the kind old white lady—"Ma'am"—Jimmy led me out the door and down several streets. "I hope that old lady doesn't get the urge to call the cops," he said, wiping his face with a polka-dotted handkerchief.

"She seemed on our side," I said. "Man, you were quick!"

Jimmy grinned. "Hey, I'm big, little girl—but I'm *spry*. You hungry?"

I wasn't, but he sure was, digging into a plate of fried chicken in a place called Maggie's. If it was Maggie herself cooking behind the counter, she sure had a forest of arm hair.

"How did you meet Basie?" I asked, taking a nibble of chicken.

Chewing loudly, Jimmy swallowed. "I was in Big 'Un's band—the Blue Devils. Man, we were good—but we were *starving*. In '29 I had a chance to jump ship and join a more prosperous band, led by a dude named Bennie Moten. So I did. Basie was playing piano for Bennie." Another piece of chicken disappeared.

"Does Big 'Un hold a grudge?"

"Nah—after a spell, he jumped ship, too. It's basic," he declared, holding a piece of chicken like a professor's ruler, "we all have to eat."

"Yeah—you more than most."

"Damn right!"

Back at the boarding house, I was ready to head upstairs for a bath, when I saw Basie, alone in the dining room, writing a letter.

"Hey, Boss," I said. "Who you writing to?"

Basie grinned his open-hearted grin. "My mother. I try to write to her at least once a week. When I was a boy she took in washing, working at least ten hours a day, partly to pay for my piano lessons. So I send her as much money as I can and she's doing alright."

"Where does she live?" Part of me was wondering if I was intruding upon his time, but I was an inquisitive little thing.

"Red Bank, New Jersey, where I was born and raised. Did you grow up in Harlem?"

"No, in Yonkers. I haven't been in Harlem too long."

Again that calm, welcoming grin: "I guess you haven't done too badly."

I mock-punched his shoulder. "Thanks to you, Boss." I stood up. "I'm off to grab a bath while the guys are all upstairs snoring."

"Avery—"

"Yes?"

"I hated to lose Lady Day—any band leader would—but you've been doing mighty fine. Pres and I think we made the right decision in hiring you."

"Thanks, Boss."

After my bath, I took a nap. The boarding house was owned by a dead minister's wife. That evening she cooked up a fine yardbird with potatoes, green beans, and hot cornbread. We were all gathered in the dining room, digging in.

"Madame can certainly burn," said Pres.

"What in the name of Jesus does that mean?" snapped the good lady of the house, who had enough meat on her frame to rip skinny Pres in two.

"It means you're an excellent cook," said Jo, his mouth full.

"Indeed," said Pres.

"It better," said our hostess. "I haven't burned anything since my first peach cobbler when I was a child." Murmuring to herself, she ambled off to the kitchen.

"Man, she looks like Moten's mother, doesn't she?" asked Big 'Un.

I thought the food was going to fly out of Basie's mouth. "You dog, I was thinking the same thing!"

"A repeater pencil," said Pres.

"Jimmy was just telling me about him," I said.

Basie sure looked sad. "Old Bennie died three years ago. Just went into the hospital to have his tonsils removed." The table was silent for a moment. I could hear the minister's widow humming a hymn in the kitchen. "This band basically grew out of Bennie's band—and Big 'Un's, too."

"I told the girl all about that, too," said Little Jimmy. By the way he was digging in, you would have thought that I'd dreamed up his fried chicken snack.

Swallowing his food, Big 'Un smiled proudly. "*Walter Page's Blue Devils*—and we were pretty fine, too, if I do say so myself."

"Once a Blue Devil," murmured Pres, "always a Blue Devil."

"I heard you in Oklahoma City in '31," said Jo, "and you cats were swinging your *asses* off!"

"Old Pres was a Blue Devil," said Lester. "You, too, Holy Main."

"Who's *Holy Main*?" I asked. Keeping up with Pres' talk could make a girl's head twirl.

Lester pointed his fork at Basie. "Holy Main is Holy Main."

Now I was absolutely confused. "But weren't you in Bennie Moten's band, Boss?" I asked.

Basie nodded. "I was—*after* I was a Blue Devil. Both Big 'Un and I joined Bennie because he was making records and the Blue Devils only made one. What year did you join Moten, Big 'Un?"

"Thirty two," said Big 'Un. "Damn Moten kept stealing my musicians one by one until I decided to throw in the towel and join him myself."

"But we're all in the Count Basie Orchestra now," said Sweets, "and we have two shows to play tonight, so we better hustle."

"Two shows?" I asked.

Buck stood up. "One for the white folks at eight, and then another for our people at eleven."

I was nineteen years old: The idea of playing two shows in one night sounded like fun—and it was.

A black girl born in 1919, I'd been called a *nigger* before. I wasn't naïve. Yet I had also been treated kindly by some white folks. The music teacher who had most encouraged me to sing, Miss Leibfred, had been a kind white lady from New Rochelle.

But I wasn't quite ready for Memphis, Tennessee.

Our second show of the night completed, I hustled back to our boarding house, naturally in the black part of town. It was a tad shabby, its bathtub needing to be scrubbed with Ajax before I settled down my skinny behind. I could hear my friends in Dickie's room, laughing and carrying on. Once it became clear that I was not going to cook (couldn't) or sew (wouldn't), Dickie had purchased a small hot plate and some pans, and his red beans and rice were really coming along.

Even though it was past midnight, I was *not* ready for bed. Shows always left me wide awake and jazzed. I was freshly bathed, ready to explore. All of Memphis was out there, waiting to be discovered. *Beale Street Blues* was one of my mother's favorite songs, and I was curious to see it, so I headed out. The air was balmy, smelling of the Mississippi River. A few couples were out strolling, but not many. Passing the darkened shops and restaurants, passing by a few still-open bars, I cast long shadows beneath the street lamps, my feet *click-clacking, click-clacking*. God, I was a stupid girl.

"Know of any good parties tonight?" asked a sudden voice from an alleyway between two brick buildings. I'll hear that voice until my dying day.

"Nope," I said, my heart jackhammering up my throat. Foolishly, I tried the "Basie Whistle," but instant dry-mouth stopped me. I was terrified. My pace quickened—*DANGER!* my mind screamed—but he grabbed me by the throat and ripped me back into the alley before I could react.

Screaming, I screamed some more, writhing beneath his weight. I could smell the whiskey on his stinking breath. Strange—but my eyes remained locked tight. I did not want to witness my rape—or my death. *Smash! Smash!* A fist slammed twice into my face. Like a cartoon character, I saw stars—but unlike a cartoon character, I could feel my mouth filling with blood. Strangely, I began hearing the voice of my Imaginary Father, telling me to survive. "That's all that matters, girl—you surviving." My underwear was ripped down to my ankles. One thought flooded my mind: *This isn't real. This isn't real. This isn't real.* But it was—and I was on the verge of losing my virginity in an evil way I'd never forget—if I lived.

Click.

This isn't real. . . .

Click.

This isn't real. . . .

"On your feet, Cracker," said a voice—familiar but ice cold. "I said, *On your feet!*"

It was Herschel's voice. Opening my eyes, I saw my friend, a pistol in his hand, brutal hatred in his eyes. The pistol was pressed against the temple of a white man who was on his knees, his overalls down by his ankles.

"Avery—can you walk?"

After pulling up my underwear, I tried to stand. Dizzy, disoriented, I threw up—right on the head of my almost-rapist.

"Dumb bitch," he muttered.

Bam! Herschel whipped the pistol against his cheek and he fell, unconscious.

"Did I give you permission to speak, Cracker?" hissed Herschel, aiming a tremendous kick into the man's groin. Even unconscious, he groaned.

Pulling at my friend's arm, I said, "Hersh, let's go. He might have some friends nearby."

Herschel's eyes seemed to return from a long distance away—a hateful (but necessary) place. "Can you walk?"

"Yes—*let's go*."

A few times when I almost fainted, my friend held me up. "You poor kid," he said, tears in his eyes. With every swallow I could taste blood. Then I must have fainted because I woke to find Herschel, breathing hard, carrying me up the boarding house stairs. "Guys!" he yelled. I was placed gently in my bed and there stood Pres, Basie, Dickie, Jo, Sweets, Buck and Big 'Un, all with anguished looks on their faces. Man, I must've looked mighty rough.

Basie phoned for a doctor, who stitched up the inside of my cheek. It hurt like hell and I began to cry. A few of my friends were on the verge of joining me.

"Were you raped, young lady?" asked the doctor, an old black gentleman with kind eyes.

"No, sir. It was close . . . but . . . no."

"I have your purse, Ave," said Herschel, the tears running down his handsome face.

Imaginary Father also had tears in his eyes. "You know I love you, girl," he said, "but you were goddamn *stupid* to go out after dark by yourself."

"I know," I whispered.

"Excuse me?" asked the doctor.

"Nothing."

"Are you going to contact the authorities, Mister Basie?"

"Should we?" asked Basie.

"No—don't," I said.

"Why?" asked the doc.

"Hersh pistol-whipped the dude. . . ."

"I kicked him in the nuts, too," added Herschel.

"How did you happen to be there?" asked the doctor.

"I saw the girl leaving the house," said Hersh, "and I knew it was Memphis past midnight, so . . . I followed her."

The doctor sighed. "If it was one of our boys even *looking* at a white girl, the rope would be bloody by now."

A needle sank into my arm and the last thing I saw was Basie's face, his wide eyes filled with concern, looking down at me. "Sleep well, dear girl," he said, planting a kiss on my forehead.

The last thing I heard as I drifted off was Pres' voice: "The South can be a stone-cold *bitch*, Lady Ave. Better not forget."

Nine

But the South could also be beautiful. Savannah, Georgia was filled with Spanish moss dripping from its trees, carriages rolling through its shady streets. Old pillared mansions had shady verandas with elderly white ladies fanning themselves and thick, mysterious gardens (and centuries of secrets) in the back.

Basie and Little Jimmy had gone to play the ponies at a race track on the outskirts of town. Basie had practically begged me to go, but I simply wanted to be alone.

"Are you okay?" he asked, those eyes boring into mine.

"I'm *fine*, Boss," I said, kissing him on the cheek. "I just want to take a walk by myself."

"Tonight's show doesn't begin until ten. I want you *back* at the hotel by *dark*. You understand?"

A kiss on his other cheek. "Yes, Dad. I understand."

Of course, I felt it terribly unfair that the guys could take late-night strolls all they wanted—but I couldn't. Unfair—but true. Yet there was plenty of humid sunshine for me to stroll around in, and Savannah was a walker's delight. Rich, pungent flowers filled every breath. I was glad we were playing four shows over two nights in this lovely town.

Was it because I was so young—or because I wasn't actually raped? All I know is that I bounced back quickly. Several vicious nightmares woke me up with the cold sweats, but overall I was fine. My Basie brothers were now over-protective, but it made me feel loved.

On this warm morning, I passed by a café and heard a familiar voice, talking (on and on), rather like a black Popeye: It was Papa Jo. Like I said, he was a professor of jazz, with *kiddies* in almost every town and city we visited. To the drummers, he gave lessons; to the other musicians he gave lectures: "Our music is *sacred*, gentlemen," he was now telling a gaggle of star-struck young cats. "We follow in the tradition of those who came before us—so you have to *take care of the temple*. Watch your liquor—drink little or *none*. Don't smoke—it clogs up the throat. It ain't good for chimneys, and it ain't good for you. And stay away from those narcotics. Pres calls drug addicts *needle dancers,* and that's all you need to know about those sad cats. They're not living for their music—they're living for that needle—and that ain't *no way* for a musician to live."

Back in school I'd learned about Socrates, teaching the young cats in the gardens of ancient Greece—and that's who Papa Jo reminded me of. He was the Socrates of Jazz.

By early afternoon I was sitting on a bench in a shady public park by the Savannah River, sipping a Coke, watching the horses pull the tourists along. Not seeing any *Whites Only* signs, I figured I was safe.

After a few moments of peace, an elderly woman walking hesitantly with a cane approached, plopping herself on the same bench. She had beautifully wrinkly mahogany skin.

"You're a young one," she said, smoothing her skirt. I hadn't even seen her glance at me.

"Yes, ma'am—1919 vintage."

"Clever, too."

"Not always," I said.

"My mama always told me I was born on a stormy February night in 1850. I'm eighty-eight years old—and I mean *old*."

"Honestly, I thought you were around 70." I was lying. She actually looked every second of eighty-eight.

"Don't lie to a liar, girl," she said, chuckling.

A thought occurred to me. "So you were fifteen when the Civil War ended. Were you a slave?"

Nodding, she said, "Yes, I was born into slavery, if that's what you mean. But my papa always told us children that we were *people*—not nobody's slaves. Of course, this was hard to believe after Papa and I were sold away."

A breeze shook the leaves far above us. "How old were you?"

"Eight." Her eyes were brown and not at all afraid to bore into mine. "My mama and my brothers stayed here in Savannah while Papa and I were sold down to Florida. You should have heard the screaming. Are you a singer?" she suddenly asked.

"How did you know?"

"There's a picture of Count Basie and you and a few others in today's paper. You're prettier than your picture."

Old folks are not afraid to tell the truth.

"Thanks—I guess. My name is Avery—Avery Hall."

"My name is Charlotte—Charlotte Davis."

I shook her warm, soft hand. *This hand did slave-work*, I thought to myself. "Did you ever see your mother and brothers again?"

Another horse-drawn carriage, filled with white tourists, rolled past. The horse must have just done its business.

"Yes, but it took years. When Papa and I were freed, our last owner—who was not a cruel man—gave us two horses and a bit of cash. We rushed on back here to Savannah, bursting with joy to see Mama and my brothers—but our first owner had by now sold *them*. At first the old weasel didn't want to say where, but Papa grabbed a bull-whip and threatened to bleed the living life out of him. I pass by that old devil's home every day—it's all boarded up and rotten now, like his soul.

"Almost soiling his pants, he told us that my baby brother had died of scarlet fever, but that he'd sold Mama and my other brother James to a plantation in Augusta. So off we galloped to Augusta. It took days—sleeping in barns, eating what we could grab. Occasionally a friendly soul would offer us a meal. Papa and I didn't talk much, but we weren't grim— just determined and a heap of afraid. Because what if they had moved? Or were dead? A lot could happen to folks back then—most of it just plain evil. So our hope was also mingled with . . . I guess *dread* is the right word.

"Finally, we reached Augusta. After a spell of asking around—my mama's name was Daisy—we finally found them, living in a tiny lean-to in the woods." The old woman's eyes filled with tears. "You never seen or heard such carrying on. Mama leapt up into Papa's arms, and then she almost smothered me in kisses. James, who is still alive, had grown so much and poor Mama looked so much older."

"How much time had passed?" I asked.

"Eight years. But my Papa found a job as a blacksmith in Augusta and we had a *life*—a *tough* life, understand, but at least a life. When we heard from a friend that the old devil had finally died, Papa figured it was safe to return to Savannah. Been here ever since."

By now we were both looking up into the warm blue sky as we spoke. Talking to this old lady was as easy as singing.

"What did you do here?" I asked.

"I'm a seamstress," she said proudly. "Had my own shop—

dresses, gowns, blouses—you name it, I can make it. Found a good man—he's dead now—and we had three sons of our own. They're all grown—all skilled working men. I see them and my grandbabies every day." Suddenly, she switched gears: "You know, I was hearing your jazz music close to forty years ago."

This was news to me. I'd thought that jazz began in the early 20s, with King Oliver, Sidney Bechet and Jelly Roll Morton.

"Yup—it's true. Must've been around 1900 I saw a poster saying that a trumpeter named Buddy Bolden was coming to town with his band. Said he was from New Orleans. I'd just finished a big job for a rich lady and had a few extra coins jingling around, so my husband and I went to hear him."

At that time I'd never heard of Buddy Bolden. King Oliver, Louis Armstrong's mentor, was the earliest trumpet player I knew. In 1938 Armstrong had himself a big band that was blazing all over the land. Buck and Sweets worshipped him the way ministers worship God.

"Was Buddy Bolden good?" I asked, just to be polite.

"Oh, yes, indeed. Played in a band shell down by the river. Had a drummer, a banjo player, and a tuba player. That man's trumpet cut clean into my soul. Handsome, too." She chuckled. "My husband was mighty lucky that I didn't trot my old bones off that night."

From down the street I could see a smoothly moving pork-pie hat heading our way. It was Pres. Wearing sunglasses and a rumpled suit, he seemed out of place—like a Harlem hipster thrust into a Civil War photograph. He smiled when he saw us.

"Lady Avery—jiving with the local beauty." Charlotte lit up like a candle as he sat down beside her on the bench.

"This is Mr. Lester Young," I said. "Lester, this is Charlotte."

After they shook hands, Pres gently kissed the old lady's hand.

"Hmm. . . ," she said, a bit flustered, "I remember years ago hearing the Young Family Band at an outdoor show in Atlanta."

Pres puffed with pride. For once the jive-talk had vanished. "That was my daddy's band. My childhood was spent in that band. Now what year would that have been, Madame?"

Charlotte closed her eyes. "Oh, maybe 1919."

"Well, I would've been playing drums back then. My daddy was a hard taskmaster—especially for learning how to read music—but he sure gave me an education."

"Nothing wrong with that, young man."

Pres was emphatic: "*No*, ma'am." Reaching into his jacket pocket, he pulled out his small bottle of witch hazel and three cotton balls. "Would you ladies like to partake in some witch hazel? Clears up those greasies."

"Are you saying that I'm *greasy*, young man?" asked Charlotte.

"On the contrary—you glow with sweet Savannah sweat, ma'am. But a little witch hazel will freshen you right up."

What a sight—a beautiful old lady, an embarrassed young lady, and a Harlem hipster, all rubbing cotton balls across our noses and foreheads! I have to admit, though, that witch hazel *is* refreshing, and whenever I smell it, I think of dear Pres.

Soon it was time to return to our latest boarding house to rest up, eat and prepare for that night's show. Saying my goodbyes to Charlotte, I offered her tickets.

"Bless you, girl, but I'm asleep these days by eight o'clock. But I'll keep my ears open about you folks—bet I'll be hearing nothing but good things."

I was truly loving this life—traveling, seeing new sights, meeting people like Charlotte. The good definitely outweighed the bad.

Ten

As we traveled deeper into the South, all the shows were segregated. Either our folks were relegated to the balcony, while the white folks milled below, or we played two shows a night: an early show for the whites, and a later, more freewheeling show for our people.

The Basie Band seemed to bring a spiritual comfort and a sense of true pride to our people. We all looked sharp—the men in their crisp blue suits, gleaming black shoes, and me in Billie's gown. We all exuded confidence and pride in our music, which by this point was cooking on all cylinders. Man, when that band was swinging the blues after midnight in some Southern ballroom, the couples slow dancing, the lights low and glittery, you felt that you were in church—a new type of free, fun, no sermonizin' church.

"*Sent for you yesterday/And here you come today*," sang Little Jimmy, the perspiration flowing off his handsome face. "*Don't the moon look lonesome/Shining down through the trees.*"

"Yes, it does, Jimmy," some lady—always a lady—would reply, wherever we were—in a barn in Tennessee, a ballroom in Dallas, or a steamy theater in Oklahoma City.

Yes: a Blues Church. That perfectly describes Count Basie's band in 1938.

And off-stage I possessed a gang of loud, teasing, loving brothers. Dickie had purchased more pots and pans, as well as a larger hot plate, and his room was always Action Central. His favorite dish was ham hocks and collard greens, but I especially dug his red beans and rice, simmering for hours after a show. Too hyped up to sleep, we would gather in Dickie's room, the boys passing around a jar of some local brew, and we'd all dig in for all we were worth. The conversation was always laid-back and easy, and I felt such warmth, such love from these musicians, that the memory always brings tears to my eyes. I loved the Boss and my Basie brothers.

"We'll be spending a week in New Orleans," said Basie one morning in a Florida diner. I was inhaling my eggs and bacon. "You eat like a football player, girl," he said, his eyes shining.

"Hanging out with you bunch makes a lady hungry. Why are we staying a week?"

"Found a place that wants to book us for a week. Ever been to New Orleans?"

"Boss, I'd never been out of New York State before I stepped on the Blue Goose." The coffee here was as good as Big Joe's. I'd seen my first palm tree the day before and all was well with the world.

Basie smiled his warm, good-hearted smile. "With your appetite, girl, you are going to love, love, *love* New Orleans."

"Baby Pres was born in Woodville, Mississippi," said Pres, "but he lived in New Orleans until he was ten."

"Almost interesting," said Hersh.

For two months we'd been swinging and swerving through the South—Georgia, Alabama, Mississippi, Florida—mostly playing one-nighters in little po-dunk towns. Most nights we played two shows—and I've already told you why.

"And wait until you try out that good old New Orleans *food!*" said Jimmy, who wasn't called *Mister Five By Five* for nothing. Closing his eyes, he almost moaned: "Red beans and rice, jambalaya, crawfish pie, soft shell crab po-boys, all *kinds* of gumbo, okra stew, barbecued shrimp, crawfish boil, black beans with Creole hot sauce, Cajun meatloaf, crab cakes, oyster pie, marinated crab salad, key-lime pie, praline pie, and more red beans and rice. My *God!*"

"Control yourself, Big Boy," said Herschel.

"*Mon Dieu,*" murmured Pres, who looked half asleep. "Pres has *big eyes* for all you're laying down. Can I interest anyone in some witch hazel?"

Basie, too, seemed lost in a New Orleans daydream. "Avery, I'll take you to the *Café du Monde*. They're open twenty-four hours a day and their coffee is *killin'*."

"Man, don't forget their beignets," added Dickie.

"What are they?" I asked.

Now it was Dickie's turn to close his eyes. "French doughnuts—like fat cruellers—served up warm with powdered sugar on top."

Jimmy sighed. "You're *hurtin'* me, man!"

Laughter rocked the diner. A few customers glanced over, but we didn't care.

My brothers were not exaggerating.

To me, New Orleans is a European city picked up and plopped down in the tropics. In the French Quarter the streets are narrow, filled with antique shops and bars and nightclubs and bizarre voodoo shops with skulls in the windows. Music is everywhere—all kinds, too: jazz, blues, Cajun fiddling, even some of that country blues. Most of the buildings have second- and third-floor balconies with railings of delicate wrought iron.

I like to look at the details of life, and I never saw a New Orleans railing that was like its brother. Each one is unique. And many of the railings are covered in flowering plants. You better be careful, because the folks who live up there love to water those plants. I saw a painted-up girl in high heels, with her breasts fairly popping out of her dress, get absolutely drenched beneath someone's balcony. Shimmying out of the way, she wailed, "*Can I get any wetter?*" I knew not to laugh, because her pimp was probably close by, with a shiv in his boot.

Next to singing on stage with Basie's band, my biggest joy was being alone, walking through another town, another village, another city, (although always now during the day). *Remember this moment, Avery,* I'd tell myself. *You might never be here again.* Yet walking around New Orleans early on an April morning, I was also thinking: *Oh, girl, you'll be here again. You'll make sure of it.*

When we hit a new town—almost daily—my routine was the same: Open my trunk, place my toothbrush and hairbrush on the dresser, check out my laundry situation, and then take a walk. It was my chance to evaluate my last performance, to mentally prepare myself for the next, to clean out my mind.

The Blue Goose had rolled into New Orleans past four in the morning. After grabbing a boarding house bath, I soon found myself on a bench, counting six bells from St. Louis Cathedral, watching the sun rise over the Mississippi. The river was wide and still, filled with early morning fire. Even in late April, the air was warm and thick, like a humid gumbo. One lone barge headed down river, towards the bend that gives New Orleans its nickname: *The Crescent City*. I could smell freshly cut grass and river water. For a spell, I was the only one about. Then I saw an elderly black man—bald as an egg, dressed in a bright red t-shirt, carrying a shoebox—slowly approaching.

Just keep on walking, Old Man, I thought to myself—but of course he didn't.

Placing the cardboard box down at my feet, he took a deep breath. "I am the human jukebox," he said, his eyes on the ground. "I can impersonate many different singers." Another deep breath: "Louis Armstrong, Little Jimmy Rushing, Robert Johnson, Lonnie Johnson, Son House, Cab Calloway, Bing Crosby, and Charley Patton." The poor old guy didn't have a tooth in his head and he obviously found his raggedy, filthy tennis shoes fascinating.

"You can impersonate Jimmy Rushing, sir?" I asked.

"Yes, indeed. My Little Jimmy choices are. . . ." Another deep breath: ". . . *Sent For You Yesterday; Goin' to Chicago; Can't Believe You In Love With Me; Evenin'*; and *Good Morning, Blues.*"

I don't like lording it over people, never have—(especially a bald old man carrying a shoebox)—so I didn't tell him that I knew Jimmy. I simply said, "How about *Good Morning, Blues*."

"Fine choice, Missy." With his old eyes shut tight, he sang a lovely, heartfelt version of Jimmy's song. The sun had risen over the treetops across the river. Shielding my eyes with my hand, I watched his dignified old face as he sung. He didn't sound a whit like Jim, but he sounded like *himself*—a cool old dude. (Come to think of it, the first time I heard the word *cool* being thrown around to mean *hip* was from Pres' lips).

You've found yourself a fine life, girl, I thought to myself. *Right now you could be serving coffee back at Big Joe's, but nope: You're sitting by the Mississippi River in New Orleans, watching the sun rise, listening to a cool old dude singing.*

The old gentleman cleared his throat. "You have one more choice on your human jukebox," he said. I chose Louis Armstrong and he tackled *When You're Smiling*. He didn't sound at all like Pops, but it was fine. Finished, he put out a wrinkled hand and I slapped a dollar into it. "Thank you kindly, Missy." Gently placing the buck into his shoebox, he slowly wandered off in search of another customer. Soon I did some wandering myself, in search of a phone booth. Finding one, I plopped in almost five dollars' worth of dimes, listening as the number rang and rang, until. . . .

"What?"

"Ted—get my mother."

I heard a curse and then: "It's for you—your daughter. She's lucky I didn't press charges."

My mother said something snappy, then took the phone: "Baby?"

We spoke for about ten minutes. To be honest, I forget most of our conversation. I was tempted to tell her about the Memphis attack, but decided to keep it to myself.

"I'm in New Orleans, Mama—right by the Mississippi River. It's as wide as the Hudson."

"Will you *shut the hell up?*" she yelled. "*I'm trying to talk to my daughter*!" I heard a door slam, then: "Sorry, baby. He's in a bad mood today."

I was so disgusted that I simply wanted to end the call. Making up some excuse, I hung up as quickly as I could. You know, I don't recall if I told her I loved her. I hope I did—but I honestly can't remember.

Nearby was the *Café du Monde*, with its green-and-white striped awnings and the wonderful smell of coffee. It was always a bit tricky down South back then, but I sat down at a table, and when the young white waitress didn't throw me out, I knew I was in.

"Try our *beignets*," she suggested, "hot out of the oven." (In case you're ever in New Orleans, they're pronounced *ben-yays*).

"As good as I've heard?" I wasn't in the mood for something crawfishy or filled with alligator meat early in the morning.

"Trust me," she said, strolling off.

Man, that waitress wasn't kidding! Three warm doughnuts, coated in powdered sugar, were placed in front of me. "Now be sure to dunk 'em in your coffee," she said, setting down the greatest cup of coffee in the universe.

Sitting at the window, watching the early artists setting up their canvases across the street in Jackson Square, I saw Basie walk past, postcards in his hand. A few knocks on the window brought him right back.

"You have to try these," I said.

"Oh, I've been in New Orleans before," he said, sitting down at my table. "I'll have a cup of coffee, too, ma'am," he said to the waitress.

I couldn't stop stuffing beignets in my mouth. Basie chuckled. "You eat those every morning, girl, and pretty soon you won't fit into your gown."

"Ah, Sweets says I'm too skinny anyways."

A few customers gave the old eye to the black man and black girl at the table, but no one said anything. Catching my eye then looking away, Basie studied a horse and carriage rolling past the café. I suddenly realized how shy this good-hearted man was.

"Who are the postcards for?" I asked.

Still watching the carriage, he said, "They're all for my mama. She lives in Red Bank, New Jersey. I'm sorry—have I already told you that?"

"No," I said, telling a lie. (I hate when people say, *You already told me that*).

"Every now and again she'll come to New York to hear the band. I'll introduce you sometime."

"Most people think you're from Kansas City, Boss."

"Nope—I'm a Red Bank boy. My parents, though, hailed from Virginia. They moved up after their marriage." He looked at me with those kind, wide-spaced eyes. "I think I've told you this, but my mother took in washing—mostly from well-to-do white folks. Sometimes she'd do some freelance cooking, too. My daddy, who's passed, was a gardener for rich white folks. Sometimes he'd be a caretaker, too—watch over those big old summer houses when the rich folks returned to the city."

I took a sip of my coffee—New Orleans coffee is delicious beyond belief. "Did you play piano as a kid?"

Basie wiped away some powdered sugar from his lips. "At first drums—but my buddy Sonny was so good on those babies that I switched to piano. My parents paid for lessons and I picked it up pretty quickly. Now how about *you*?" Basie had the gift of making you feel important. (If you've noticed, many folks do *not*).

"What about me?"

"You've been singing up a storm and the guys all love you like a little sis. You feel like staying with us for a while?"

Stay cool, I told myself. "Sure. Beats waitressing."

Basie grinned. "We have a record date as soon as we return to New York and I'd like to have you record a song or two."

"A record!" This is what I'd been secretly hoping—what almost every girl hoped in 1938: to hear her voice spilling out of jukeboxes and radios and people's apartments.

"So that's a *yes*?" asked Basie, peering at me over his coffee cup.

"Yup!"

For the next few seconds, Basie had trouble making eye contact. For that matter, so did I.

"What happened in Memphis. . . ." He paused. "How are you?"

I stared down into my coffee. "Fine. I've pushed it out of my mind. Mostly." I looked up. "Of course, it would be worse if I'd been raped. But I wasn't—thanks to Hersh."

"He was following you on purpose, you know. It wasn't just luck."

I had actually forgotten this. For several weeks I was convinced that I'd been saved by a happy coincidence. Instead, I realized I'd been saved by a caring friend.

Basie coughed. "There are two types of men in this world, Avery. The ones like me—and the rest of the guys—could not rape a woman the same way we could not jab a fountain pen in our ear." I winced. "Then there's the type of dog who could do it in a heartbeat—and not feel *one second* of remorse." Sounding exactly like Imaginary Father, he added: "That type is the minority—but they're out there. All I'm saying is—be careful."

I rested my hand on top of his. "I will. Thanks, Boss."

After paying—Basie was always an extravagant tipper—we crossed Decatur Street and strolled through early morning Jackson Square. The bells of St. Louis (Armstrong!) Cathedral rang seven times.

"Can I ask you a personal question, Ave?"

"Another one?"

Basie chuckled. "Yeah—and here goes: Every other girl singer I've hired sooner or later falls for one of the guys. There are a couple of them who wouldn't mind falling in love with *you*. How come you play it so cool?"

I'd been thinking of this myself. Herschel and Jimmy were married, so they were out of bounds, and Pres was simply too out there—but Buck or Sweets or even intense Jo were handsome, available men. Why wasn't I interested?

"I don't know, Boss. I grew up watching my mother fall for one loser after another. I've even seen her get smacked around. I guess it's made me kind of careful—and I'm in no hurry. You know what I mean? I like just being *me*—alone and not having to answer to anyone." Basie was smiling. "Now don't get me wrong—I want to meet someone *someday* to get married and all of that. But . . . right now . . . I'm simply happy being inside myself, taking it all in."

We stopped walking. Wrapping me in his strong arms, my boss kissed me lightly on the forehead. "Sometimes I dream of having a daughter. Never a son—always a daughter. And when she grows up, I hope she's a lot like you."

I loved Count Basie.

Eleven

The Suburban Gardens was a spacious, ramshackle ballroom by the Mississippi River. It had no air-conditioning and smelled of years of dancers' sweat and stale bayou. Backstage was shadowy and as humid "as a gorilla's armpit," according to Dickie, who was oiling his trombone.

After dressing in the single-toilet bathroom, I stood around listening to the sounds, the coughs and easy laughter of the audience.

"Pace yourself," said Basie. "This first one is for the white folks—later on for our own people."

Finding a wooden crate to sit on, I was hoping my behind wasn't about to collect splinters.

"Pops was here back in '31," said Jo, chomping on his spearmint gum.

"Louis Armstrong?" I asked.

"Yup—it was a radio broadcast and at the last moment the white radio boy said, 'I just can't announce this nigger.'"

"You're kidding," I said.

"Wish I was. So Pops strides up to the microphone, says in his bullfroggy voice, 'Give me a chord,' and announces the show himself. Must've been beautiful."

Herschel was tying his shoes. "That was the first time a black man's speaking voice was heard on the radio down here." Hersh had been looking a tad tired lately—but then again, the constant bumping around the South on the Blue Goose left us *all* tired *all* the time.

Back in his hometown, Pres was on fire that night, weaving complex yet airy solos. His eyes closed, his horn tilted, he seemed to be in another universe altogether—the universe of instant creativity. Despite his hangdog look, Herschel was not too far behind, blowing some mighty solos that had the dancers stomping. This evening, too, I really watched and listened to Dickie—the eerie sounds he coaxed out of his trombone were something to hear. And above it all, chewing his gum *rat-ta-tat-tat*, like the King of Rhythm himself, sat Papa Jo, smiling down on his kiddies.

If the first show was magnificent—and it was—then the evening's second show was beyond the beyond. Maybe it was because our people had stood waiting in a misty rain for the first show to end; maybe it was because we were in New Orleans, the sacred birthplace of jazz; but whatever the cause, the Basie band played the hottest, most driving show I've *ever* experienced. Period. Picking up the spirit, I really leaned into my songs, practically shrieking at the climax of *Basin Street Blues*. It's hard to explain, but I simply felt so free that all constraints were tossed out the window and floating downriver. It's too bad you weren't born yet—you would've enjoyed yourself.

After the second show, I grabbed myself a Coke from an ice-filled bucket and was sitting in the dark, collecting myself, when I saw Herschel fall to one knee. Thinking that he was praying, I was ready to give him his privacy, when he fell onto his side.

"Hersh! You alright?" No one else was around.

Climbing back onto one knee, Herschel grinned. "Just a little chest pain. I think my suitcase is getting too heavy and I grabbed it too quickly this morning." A chewing gum wrapper was stuck with sweat to the side of his face. Gently, I removed it.

"I'll tell Basie. You might need a doctor."

Slowly standing up, Herschel dusted off the knees of his pants. "Don't be crazy, Ave. I'm fine. Just a little dizziness, that's all."

That night some local musicians threw a no-holds-barred party for the Basie Band on Frenchmen Street, but I grabbed a taxi with Hersh and headed back to the boarding house. After making sure that he showered and brushed his teeth, I tucked him into bed.

"I heard the Boss say there's no need for rehearsal tomorrow. So you sleep in late, Hersh, you hear?"

My friend grinned his handsome grin. "Yes, indeed, ma'am. You know, I never had a bossy younger sis—but I certainly do now."

I kissed Herschel on the forehead; he felt cool. "No talking, mister—just sleep."

Right before I closed the door he said: "Ave?"

"Yeah?"

"Don't tell anyone—okay?"

I didn't think before answering; I was young.

"Okay, Hersh."

"Thanks, Sis."

And I kept my word.

Wish I hadn't.

The weeks swung by. We worked our way up North by playing yet another string of one-nighters: Dallas, Texas (where we all met Herschel's parents—a lovely, quiet couple); Tulsa, Oklahoma; Wichita, Kansas; Kansas City, Missouri (you wouldn't *believe* the party the town threw for the band!); St. Louis, Missouri; Louisville *and* Lexington (again), Kentucky; Pittsburgh, Pennsylvania; Cleveland, Ohio; Buffalo, New York; and a swing down to Hartford, Connecticut.

Herschel had just played a version of *Blue and Sentimental* that made the dancers sigh when it happened: Our friend crumpled to the floor of the stage. Surprisingly for a large man, Big 'Un flashed over first, cradling Herschel's head. He was unconscious; the edge of the saxophone had cut his cheek.

"Is there a doctor in the house?" called Basie from the lip of the stage.

There was—a beautiful black lady—and she rushed up, checking for a pulse in Herschel's neck. "Call an ambulance," she said.

It may sound cruel, but the show continued after Herschel was taken away, still unconscious, on a stretcher. It certainly wasn't a swinging performance. Both Pres and Jo had tears running down their faces and the rest of us had tears standing in our eyes.

At 2:30 in the morning the entire band was crammed into the waiting room of the hospital. Strange, but this was my first time ever being in one—and I couldn't get over the odd smell. My mama had brought me to several doctors' offices, but never (and this is probably a good thing) to a hospital.

Finally a doctor—not the lady from the theater, but a white man—stepped out.

"Is there any kin here?" he asked.

"His wife's in New York," said Basie. "I'm calling her tomorrow morning. I'm his boss."

"Well," said the doctor, looking at all of us. "It's not a heart attack—yet—but your friend has a heart condition. He's going to need a great deal of rest. I'd tell his wife as soon as possible."

"Didn't you hear the man?" snapped Jo. "He'll call her tomorrow morning."

Poor Pres sat alone in a chair, away from the rest of us. His already sad eyes looked far off, shattered. I thought how the music magazines all made it sound as if he and Herschel were musical enemies—rivals out to cut each other every night. The truth was that they were brothers.

About an hour later I found myself in a quiet bar with Pres and Jo. I was sipping an iced tea, but Pres was on his third glass of rye whiskey. On the jukebox, Louis Armstrong was gently singing, *I'm Confessin'*.

Jo's eyes for once did not look jolly; he was chomping on his Wrigley's Spearmint with even more vigor than usual. "I remember back in Kansas City, Pres, all you drank was milk."

"Them days are gone with the wind, Lady Jo," said Pres, staring into his glass.

Pounding his chest like a chief, Jo was angry. "Man, you're a *jazz musician*, Pres—one of the greatest I've ever heard. Other tenormen base their *careers* on trails you've blazed. Don't you know the *gift* we've all been given? We get to play our music and make people happy—take them away from the dust of their lives. We bring *joy*, man, wherever we go. How many people can say they bring joy in their jobs? Precious few. You're a great musician, Pres—*respect the temple.*"

Muttering something about gray boys, Pres finished his drink, put on his pork pie hat, and left us. The bell rang over the bar's door. *Bells, bells.* Poor Jo looked close to tears.

"Look at my drink, Avery—my *one* drink. I'll order one and then nurse it for an hour. And then that's *enough*—I'm finished. Why can't Pres do the same?"

I didn't know what to say. "He's not you," was all I managed.

Jo smiled. "Or you, girl. Don't think I haven't noticed. You have a good head on your shoulders."

I patted his hand. "Thanks, Jo."

And I would need that good head over the next few days.

Twelve

At first I thought that the knocking on my door was the blue jay in my dream, pecking at the side of a purple tree. When the bird didn't stop, even when I tossed an orange coconut at it, I slowly began to realize that the knocking belonged to the real world.

"One minute," I called, wrapping a bedsheet around me. "Who is it?"

"Basie."

Opening the door, I saw a stricken looking boss in the doorway.

"Is Herschel dead?" I asked.

"God, no. No, he's resting. But the police just called me, Avery. Can I come in?"

After using the bathroom to brush my teeth and put on a robe, I sat on the edge of the bed. Jittery, Basie could not stop pacing.

"What is it, Boss?"

Taking a deep breath, he said it: "Your mother was murdered yesterday by her boyfriend."

"Oh."

So there it was—as if it had all been preordained.

Of course. My mother. Murdered. By one of her boyfriends.

Naturally.

"He's not all that bad."

"You're not giving him a chance, Avery."

"You don't know him. He has a good side, too."

"You're too young to understand these things. One day you'll understand."

One day I'd understand *what*, Mama? That a woman must learn to put up with a violent, cruel, abusive creep in order to be happy?

During my childhood she had brought to our home one loser after another after another.

"You don't understand, Avery."

Maybe not. But as I sat on the edge of the hotel bed, I clearly understood one thing: My mother had been murdered by her boyfriend, Ted, who had then shot himself in his worthless head.

"Take as much time off as you need, Avery," said Basie.

My brain was a puddle of empty static. "What? Yes, sure. How's Herschel?"

Sitting down next to me, Basie wrapped me in his arms, the way Imaginary Father would have, if he were real. "He's resting. I'm going to the hospital in a few minutes. *Shh*. . . ."

I don't know how long I cried, but that good, good man did not let me go.

Later that afternoon, I stepped off a train at Penn Station. Deb was waiting.

"I know I can't say anything to make you feel better . . . but I'm sorry, Ave."

I took her hand. "Thanks, Deb. How's our apartment?"

It was cleaner than I'd ever kept it. My mail was neatly piled on my dresser. Glancing through the bills, I saw my mother's handwriting on an envelope which had been postmarked two weeks earlier. Ripping it open, I read:

Dear Baby:
I know I don't say these things too often, but I'm really proud of you. Last night on the radio I heard you singing with Count Basie from Dallas, Texas and you sounded great. That's my little girl! I said to Ted. He's proud of you, too, don't think he isn't. That's all. I just love you, Avery.
Love,
Mama

Yeah, I cried.

Naturally, Mama didn't leave any money behind. In fact, her debts totaled over eight hundred dollars—but Basie stepped in and paid them all. He even paid for the funeral, which was held on a windy sunny day. At first the only people in the Yonkers graveyard were the reverend, Debbie, a friend of Mama's named Florence, and me.

"Lord," intoned the reverend, his adam's apple struggling against his white collar. "Please accept the soul of your servant. . . ."

Christ, I thought, *Mama was the servant of liquor and worthless men, not you.* A black car pulled into the cemetery. An arm pointed out from one of the back windows, then the car headed our way.

"Please, just a second," I said.

The good reverend seemed annoyed, but then very much impressed as Count Basie, Jo Jones, Walter Page and Buck Clayton stepped out of the car, which Big 'Un had been driving, all dressed in black suits. Without saying a word, my friends embraced me, then linked arms around me.

"All set," I said.

And that was my mother's funeral.

About a week later I was moping in my apartment when someone knocked on the door. Deb didn't even look up from her books. "Can you get that, Ave?"

It was Jo and Basie, dressed up like funky zootsuiters, with zebra suspenders and hats perched at cocky angles.

"Come on, girl," said Jo, his hypnotic smile (and gum) working overtime. "Don't keep your brothers waiting."

"Where are we going?"

"To the Joe Louis fight at Yankee Stadium!" said Basie. Jo began shadow boxing, throwing imaginary punches at an imaginary foe.

"Didn't you tell her, Debbie?" asked Basie.

Deb didn't even look up from her books. "Must have forgotten, Count. Sorry."

"Let's go, girl!" said Jo.

Throwing on some slacks and a blouse, I followed my friends to the waiting cab. "Yankee Stadium, sir," said Basie to the driver.

"You got it, Count."

The windows were rolled down and Harlem was even more alive than usual. Every stoop was filled with folks, every window was opened wide, the sounds of radios spilling out. It was June 22, 1938.

"Man, two years ago, when Schmeling beat Joe, people were *crying* in the streets," said Jo.

"You were one of them," said Basie.

"Damn right. I love Joe Louis like a brother."

"You know him?" I asked.

"Our Jo knows everyone," said Basie.

Our cab had just passed the darkened Polo Grounds. Across the river, all lit up, was Yankee Stadium.

"I know Joe lost two years ago," I said, "but what exactly happened?"

Turning, the cab driver said, "That bum Schmeling kept jabbing in Joe's eye—he couldn't see. *Jab, jab, jab!*"

"Please watch the road, pal," said Basie. "But yup, that's basically it."

Jo threw an imaginary punch. "But not tonight, baby!"

When I was seven years old, one of my mother's better boyfriends had brought me to Yankee Stadium. I'd even seen Lou Gehrig hit a homerun. But that long ago afternoon was nothing like this. Huge krieg lights lit up the sky as thousands of people streamed into the stadium's many entrances.

"Hey, there's Count Basie!" I heard someone call. But Basie, his face as excited as a little boy's, said, "Hey, there's Gary Cooper!"

"There's Clark Gable!" said Jo.

"You're pulling my crank," I said, holding onto Basie's hand. If we were separated in this crowd, I'd never find them again.

"You have a crank?" asked Jo.

Our seats were close to the third base line. The stadium was lit up, bright as day, with a raucous, circus feeling in the air. It was a balmy night, very breezy, with the smell of hot dogs and cigars everywhere. Most in the crowd were white folks, but there were quite a few black folks, too—along with Asian and Hispanic folks—and everyone seemed to be getting along. Strange, but when it was American versus German, the silly color situation didn't seem to matter. (Later I would find this statement to be a dirty lie, but that's years ahead).

"Man, the Roman Coliseum must have felt like this," said Jo, gazing about.

"Jo Jones! Count Basie!" cried a voice. "When are you cats playing the Savoy again?"

Standing like a politician—or a prince—Jo said, "Soon, man—early August we'll be back swinging at the Savoy." Taking a deep breath, Jo was ready to dive into a speech, but a chorus of boos drowned him out. Max Schmeling was strolling out of the visitor's dugout, throwing punches at the air. "Go back to Germany, you dirty Nazi!" cried a voice.

"For a second there," said Jo, holding onto his hat as a gusty breeze blew past, "I thought they were booing *me*!"

"Perish the thought," said Basie, munching on peanuts.

And suddenly, there he was—Joe Louis, the *Bronx Bomber*, bounding out of the Yankee dugout. Singing with Basie, I've heard some cheering crowds in my time, but *nothing* like this. This sounded like every boom of thunder you've ever heard rounded up together—then *tripled*. Tipping an imaginary hat to the crowd, Joe, shadow boxing, headed to the ring, which was by second base.

"He's looking good," said Jo. "Check out those muscles."

"Oh, I am," I said—and Basie almost choked on his peanuts.

Soon Schmeling and Joe were in their corners, taking last minute instructions from their people. When the announcer said the name *Joe Louis*, it made the earlier ovation sound like a whisper. (When he said *Max Schmeling*, it made me hope that the man had a tank to drive him back to his hotel). Before I knew it, a bell sounded and the fight was on!

This was many years ago, but I vividly recall Joe charging Schmeling like an angry bull, throwing punch after punch. The crowd screamed.

"*Damn it to hell!*" cried a voice—Basie's. I'd never heard the man speak above a conversational tone, but another gust of wind had swept off his hat and he was on his knees, cursing and searching. Figuring the man had paid for my mother's funeral, I, too, ducked down, scrambling on the gum-and-cigarette-strewn cement floor for the hat, which was quite expensive.

"Got it!" cried Basie, his wide eyes filled with excitement. "Thanks, Ave."

Now the crowd was absolutely berserk, louder than before. It was *End of the World* crazy noisy. At first I thought the people around us were simply happy that Basie had found his hat—but the noise filled the entire stadium. Every man, woman, and child were on their feet—every man, woman, and child that is, except Max Schmeling. He was on his ass, down for the count, and Joe Louis had won—only two minutes and four seconds into the fight.

"*Did you see that?*" screamed Jo, the gum almost falling out of his mouth. "Did you *see* that?"

But we hadn't. Shrugging at each other, Count Basie and I simply joined the noise. Cupping his hand over my ear, Basie yelled, "Let's keep it to ourselves that we missed the fight."

Jo cupped *his* hand over my ear and yelled, "He must think I'm as dumb as he looks!"

It took nearly half an hour to be spilled out of Yankee Stadium. The Grand Concourse was hopping like Mardis Gras. *"JOE WON! JOE WON! JOE WON!"* chanted a group of white and black teenage boys. Basie held onto my hand.

Jostling through the crowd, we were lucky to hail a taxi a few blocks away. "999 Riverside Drive," Basie told the driver. "I'm sorry, Ave—did you want to go home first?"

"Where are we going?"

"To Herschel's apartment," said Jo. "We told him we'd drop by after the fight."

"He's out of the hospital?" I asked.

"Yesterday."

"I'm with you."

The apartment building was a light stone citadel bathed in moonlight. A leafy park stood dark across the street, with the wide, silent Hudson River beyond.

Herschel lived on the third floor. A beautiful lady dressed in blue opened the door. I was immediately jealous.

"Count! Jo! Come in, come in," she said, her smile the genuine article. "Hersh will be glad to see you. He's putting Jordan to bed."

A little girl, maybe three or four, as lovely as her mother, burst into the living room. "Uncle Jo! Uncle Bill!" she shrieked, leaping up into Jo's awaiting arms. Reaching into Jo's shirt pocket, she yanked out a package of Wrigley's Spearmint, giggling like a thief. In a yellow nightgown, with her hair in braids, she left cute a thousand miles in the dust.

In the doorway, in a blue bathrobe, painfully thin, stood Herschel. He smiled. "Thanks for dropping by, guys. Pres was here—he just left."

"Damn!" said Jo. "We missed that rascal."

Mrs. Evans, whose name was Lorraine, swooped up the little girl in her arms. "It's time for bed, darling. Give your uncles a kiss goodnight and then I'll tuck you in."

When she stood in front of me, I said, "I'm Avery. Your dad is a good friend of mine."

Looking me up and down, she said, "You're pretty. Daddy says you're a good singer who should make records."

Elbowing Basie, Jo said, "I *told* you, Bill. The girl's gonna have *hits*."

Soon we were all sitting in the living room—Herschel and Lorraine on the couch, the rest of us in comfy chairs. The radio was softly set to a classical station.

"The doc says I'll be back soon," said Herschel. "He says I'm doing fine."

Lorraine gave her husband an odd look. "That's not exactly what he said, Hersh."

"Close enough," said Herschel. "I've been practicing, guys, and the horn's sounding fine. Pres says you're making him work twice as hard with me gone."

"Just take your time," said Basie. "You *know* that you'll always have a job. So no worries there."

"We're family, Hersh," said Jo.

My friend had tears in his eyes. "I know. Thanks, guys. I just miss it so *bad.*"

Wrapping her hand in his, Lorraine put her head on her husband's shoulder and closed her eyes. At that moment I would have given my future to be her for only five minutes.

I *was* a strange girl, I admit that—but it was easy to understand why. When I saw Herschel gently kiss his daughter on her forehead, I ached for a father like him. Let's be honest: Imaginary Father was just that—imaginary. And now, seeing him holding hands with his wife, I ached for a Herschel Evans for a husband. I knew that even though he had saved me that terrible night in Memphis—which to *me* gave us a true connection—I was only a friend, nothing more. Of *course* I knew that. But seeing him in his home, with his wife and daughter, only pounded that fact more deeply into my thick head. *I guess you have to find a Herschel of your own one day*, I remember thinking.

Jo's banter kept us all laughing—especially his retelling of Basie looking for his hat and missing the fight—but we didn't stay too long. Herschel looked too exhausted. So did Lorraine.

So we said our goodbyes. When Herschel hugged me, he still smelled like Herschel—of Ivory soap with just a hint of woodsy cologne. "Love you, kid," he whispered into my ear.

"Love you, too, Hersh," I said.

And eight months later, on a gray, bone-chilling winter's day, when I saw Herschel's casket being lowered into the ground, with his wife and little daughter crying inconsolable tears, I said those same words:

"Love you, too, Hersh."

Thirteen

Man, did the years pick up speed after that. On the first of September 1939, Adolf Hitler invaded Poland and World War II began. Of course, the United States would not dive in until after December 7, 1941, but it changed the atmosphere, that's for sure.

A wonderful tenor saxophonist from Texas named Buddy joined the band after Herschel's death. He played with soul—but he was not Hersh. Something changed in Pres, too, after his brother's death. Always strange, he became stranger, more silent, more living within himself. On stage Pres was still a master, blowing ballet-dancer-like solos with his horn at a 45 degree angle—but offstage he retreated further back into his soul. His drinking increased, too, with frequent nips from a silver flask he now kept in his jacket pocket.

"Pres, you're a *jazz musician*, man," admonished Jo (again) late one night after a show. "It's a *sacred calling*, brother. What other artists create beauty out of thin air the way we do every night? *Nobody*, that's who! And because it's a sacred calling, man, you have to *respect the temple!*"

Tilting his pork pie hat lower over one eye, Pres said, "Lady Jo, I've dug your jive before. Don't you understand? A gray-boy

Bob Crosby was lurking out there tonight, shooting old Pres the evil eye, so I need some sips of my medicine, y'understand."

In October 1939, I made my first recording with the Basie Band, a little number I'd written called *Riverside Drive Blues*. To be honest, I only wrote the words, with Basie and Big 'Un creating the tune. It was a kick to walk the evening streets of Harlem with Debbie, hearing my song floating out of brownstone windows or from saloon jukeboxes. *Downbeat* magazine said: "Miss Avery Hall sings with sly wit and spirit and might even give Lady Day and Ella some competition up the road." Who was I to argue? I kept that review, you bet. Imaginary Father also kept a copy in his wallet, showing it proudly to his buddies at the factory.

One evening in Columbus, Ohio, I saw and heard Pres weeping in the darkened alley outside the theater. I knew he was thinking of Herschel, so I left him alone. Pres could sure be weird, but he was also gentle and kind, and many evenings I saw him giving extra help to Buddy, to help him learn the ways of Basie. "But remember, Lady Bud, this is *your* gig. You're not here to be a repeater pencil of Lady Hersh. You be your *own* man with your *own* ideas and your *own* sound. Originality's the thing. You can have tone and technique and a lot of other things, but without originality you ain't really nowhere. Gotta be original, man."

This time I butted in. "Hey, Pres, Sweets once told me that you had a hard time fitting in with the Fletcher Henderson band."

His eyes out for mischief, Pres' voice rose higher and higher: "*Sheeeeet!* Why did Lady Smack have to treat me so *bad*? And his *wife*—man, she was even worse than Lady Smack!" (While old Pres frets and fumes, I'll let you off the hook: the bandleader Fletcher Henderson's nickname was *Smack)*. "I had me a portable record player and one morning in Kansas City that bitch flounces in with a Coleman Hawkins record. 'Why don't you play like *this*, Pres?' she asks, all gums and bad breath. Now I *dig* Hawk—you understand? I seriously dig the man *and* his sound. *But I ain't Coleman Hawkins!* I'm *Pres*—and I have my *own* way of playing." He tapped his belly. "Hawk and Hersch play from here—deep in the belly." He tapped his temple. "But for me, I'm flying high in the old noggin'." Smiling his snaggletoothed smile, he grumbled some more: "*Sheeeeet!* Why did that bitch want to hog and dog old Pres like that? I didn't tell her to dress like Zazu Pitts, now did I?'

Poor Buddy was nodding and smiling like he was talking to a foreigner, and I wandered off, tickled to death. I sure loved to hear Lester Young talk!

However, by late 1940 Pres was gone, leaving Basie for his own small combo in L.A. Then the United States entered the war and I heard he'd been drafted, just like Papa Jo and Sweets and Freddie and Dickie and Buck. "It's lucky we're too fat," chuckled Jimmy one afternoon to Big 'Un.

"Pays to eat well, Brother Rushing," said Big 'Un, polishing his big bass.

I told myself that I'd never leave Basie—that I owed this dear man too much. But something happened at Fort Morrill, Georgia in July 1944 that made me realize I probably needed a good long rest.

By this time I'd had a few hit records and had my own share of fans. But did I do what I did because I'd grown too big for my own head?

No, I really don't think I did. But you decide:

It was as hot as Georgia in July as we rolled into Fort Morrill. D-Day—the day the Allies began snatching France back from Hitler—was five weeks in the past, and everyone was saying that the war would soon be over. I kept tabs on all my old Basie brothers, and I knew that none had yet died in battle. (Luckily, none would).

Stupidly, I assumed that we'd be playing for both black and white soldiers. We saw many black soldiers as the Blue Goose rolled slowly through the narrow streets of the base. Most smiled and waved. One young private even doffed his cap and called out, "I loved Herschel, man!" Hot tears from that.

The Fort Morrill theater was not the worst we'd played—but close to it. With a low ceiling, metal floors, and cramped restrooms, it was none too welcoming. Neither was the officer in charge, Major Gahm or something. A short red-faced turd, he looked at Basie with outright disgust.

"You boys will go on at eight o'clock *sharp*," he said. "Tardiness is not tolerated here."

Basie stared daggers at the dude. "My *men* are professionals who know how to tell time."

"Well, that's fine. Glad to hear it," said Major Gahm. "Now you asked in your letter if you'd be playing to colored soldiers. I ran it by my superiors and the answer is *no*."

"What the—?" swore Big 'Un. I'd never heard the big man curse before and it was a shock.

"Why the hell not?" asked Basie. I'd never seen the boss this angry before. It was a day of firsts.

"Number one, watch your language, *boy*," snapped Major Gahm, growing even redder in the face. "Second, be satisfied that you're playing your music in front of United States soldiers."

"Come on, Bill, let's get out of here," said Jimmy. "We don't need this garbage."

Major Gahm (or something) raised himself to his full height, which wasn't much. "You do that, boy, and I'll make sure the entire nation knows that you're unpatriotic scum who refused to play for our servicemen."

"Wait a minute," said Basie. "Big 'Un, Jimmy, Avery—over here."

Looking at his watch, the major said, "I'll give you *one minute.*"

"You can't be considering this," said Big 'Un.

"Walter," said Basie, "we're finished if we don't. Can't you picture the headlines? *Colored band refuses to play for soldiers.* All our future bookings will be canceled."

"But what about our own people?" I asked.

We locked eyes—but Basie said nothing.

"Major," said Basie, dignified as always. "We're willing to play a second show, at ten o'clock, for the black soldiers. We'll play for free."

Gahm looked as if Basie had just said, *"We're willing to kick your mama, at ten o'clock, right in the teeth. We'll do it for free."*

"I don't think you understand, *boy*," he said. "You and your *boys* are playing *one* show at eight o'clock for white United States soldiers. Is that understood?"

Knowing Basie as well as I did, I knew this was killing him. Yet he betrayed no emotion behind those placid eyes. "Yes, I understand. My *men* and I and Avery will be ready." Turning, he walked away.

So it was a grim group of musicians who took the stage that night. The theater was packed and noisy. "Those are United States soldiers out there," said Basie right before the curtain rose. "Some of those boys will be overseas dying in a few weeks. Let's remember that and play our best."

And we did. Our opening number, *Boogie Woogie*, had the soldiers on their feet, clapping their hands. Our second, *Jumpin' at the Woodside*, had many soldiers dancing in the aisles. Some lunkhead did call out, "Swing it, Fatboy!" when Jimmy sang *Sent For You Yesterday*, but what the heck—Jimmy *was* fat and he *was* swinging it.

Then it was my turn. As the band swung into *My Heart Belongs to Daddy*, I approached the microphone to a chorus of cheers and wolf whistles. Dressed in a blue gown, fresh from a backstage shower, I knew I looked rather snazzy. The band was cooking and I was really into the song, squeezing out the nuance of every word of the lyric, when it happened.

The back doors of the theater opened. Four armed military policemen led in at least ten men dressed in drab gray pajamas. Clearly, they were prisoners. Since all the seats in the theater were taken, the prisoners and MPs stood in the back. Although I was in mid-song, one part of my brain began to thinking: "*Hmm . . . they're obviously prisoners of war . . . and they're not Japanese . . . and they don't look Italian. . . .*" That left only one possibility: "*We're playing right now . . . and I'm singing to . . . Nazis!*"

When I slammed the microphone to the stage floor, it made an unholy screetch, and the band slammed to a halt. "You have *got* to be shitting me!" I shouted to no one in particular. Basie looked horrified, but Big 'Un was grinning. "We're not allowed to play to black soldiers—but *we're playing to goddamn Nazis?*"

Trying (and utterly failing) to be as lady-like as possible, I stalked off-stage. Major Gahm, appearing out of nowhere, had his finger in my chest. "Get your skinny black ass out there," he hissed.

"Get your goddamn finger out of my tits!" I yelled, shoving past him. At this point, I could hear commotion and I knew that my band mates were following me. All I had to carry was my sweet self, but I could hear Big 'Un huffing and puffing with his bass. I felt bad, but what else could I do? The soldiers were stomping their feet and making all kinds of noise. I couldn't tell if they were angry at me—or angry that the Nazis had been herded in to hear the show.

"The newspapers will hear about this!" screamed Major Gahm at Basie.

"Control yourself, man, you'll spurt," said Basie, cool as ever. "And go ahead and tell the papers. I can see the headlines now: *Basie and Band Refuse to Play for Nazis.* That's golden publicity, you sad turkey." Saluting, Basie stared him in the eye. "The Count Basie Band does not play for Nazis."

For a second I thought Gahm was going to punch Basie, but he didn't. As we left it behind, the noise from the theater was some kind of crazy. The Blue Goose was loaded up and soon we were driving through the gates of Fort Morrill. Old Sam, still our driver, chuckled as Shadow, our new drummer, told him the story. "*Get your goddamn finger out of my tits!* Avery told the dude. She was roaring like a mother lion."

I could see Sam's eyes in the rearview mirror. "You said that, girl? Good for you."

"Sam, they had us playing for *Nazis*—and our own people were not allowed to attend the show."

"Dirty sons of bitches," Sam muttered.

Seated alone, looking out the window at the dusky Georgia countryside, was Count Basie. I sat next to him. Turning, he looked me over with those wide-spaced, soulful eyes.

"I'm sorry," I said. Never having had a father, I don't know how a girl loves her dad—or feels gutted when she disappoints him—but maybe at that moment I did.

Wrapping an arm around me, he pulled me into his shoulder. Man, that cat always smelled so fine. I rested my head and closed my eyes.

"You, my girl, have nothing to be sorry about. *I'm* the one apologizing here—for not doing what you did the *second* I heard that our soldiers had been shut out."

"Love you, Avery," called a familiar voice from the back of the bus, where already a high-stakes poker game was in full swing.

"Love you, too, Jimmy."

I fell asleep that night on Count Basie's shoulder.

Fourteen

In 1945 the war ended in both Europe and the Pacific—and I left the Count Basie Orchestra. After seven years of living out of a trunk, sleeping on the Blue Goose, or surviving yet another boarding house with a rusty bathtub down the hall, I was plum exhausted.

"You can come back at *any* time, Ave," said Basie, wrapping me in his arms. "You know that, girl."

Debbie, now a full-fledged nurse, had met a good man named Kai. I sang at their wedding and a year later Kai Junior popped into view. Naturally, I wasn't going to kick newlyweds out of my old West 145th Street digs, so I packed up my few belongings and moved into a small but fine apartment in Greenwich Village. I lived on the third floor and from my bedroom window I looked out on peaceful, leafy, bird-filled Patchen Place. On most days a bald man set up his easel down below to paint colorfully bold pictures of birds and sky.

Thanks to Basie's generosity, my thriftiness (and a few hit records—you've heard *The Fort Georgia Blues*, haven't you?), I had no money worries. I took long walks through my new neighborhood, learning the twisty streets and cafes and bookstores of the Village. I'm sure that people saw the woman sitting by herself in a café, reading a book, and thought, *Poor lonely soul.* But honestly, I was never lonely. After living on a bus with a gaggle of men for seven years, it felt good to be alone, to answer to no one. I wasn't even tempted to sing.

So for two years you can say I just kind of floated—and healed. A few of my friends worried about me, but I knew I was fine. More than fine, actually.

Living within yourself can be comforting—but it can't last forever. During my cocoon time, did I think often of my mother? Of course—and I did cry for her—but I found myself thinking of (and crying for) Herschel much more often. I tried to analyze why—and the answer was so simple it was brutal: Hersh had been kinder to me. With my poor mother, her men and her liquor had always come first—even when I was a child. Herschel, on the other hand, had cared enough for me to follow me that night in Memphis. My mother would have stayed inside with her latest craze.

Like I said—brutal.

One crisp October evening in 1947 I saw a sign outside the Village Vanguard: *Tonight! Lester Young and his Quartet!* Paying my few bits, I walked down the stairs, finding a seat at the bar in the back. I hadn't seen Pres in over four years and he looked thinner, his suit baggy and in need of pressing. But his long hair still scraggled over the back of his collar and that pork pie hat was still set at a rakish angle.

Sipping a glass of wine, I closed my eyes and dreamed to Pres' music. Dear Herschel always played solos that reminded me of muscle, rich soil, real life. But Pres' solos always seemed to drift on a turquoise cloud somewhere in Dreamland. His band consisted of a pianist, bassist, and drummer, none of whom I knew. They did their job admirably, keeping out of the way and allowing my Lester to play his dreams.

I stayed for both sets, utterly enchanted, and when the evening was over, Pres was surrounded by well-wishers and fans. Naturally, he talked his crazy talk, the lonely Pilgrim of Cool. When he saw me, still seated at the bar, our eyes locked for a long while, and the well-wishers were forgotten.

"Well, well, well . . . Lady Ave," he muttered, strolling over to me in his soft crepe shoes, still smelling of a fresh shave and witch hazel. Taking my hand, he gently kissed it. "A startled doe indeed."

"You need to eat more, my friend," I said, "and probably drink less."

"Ah, man, you know. . . . The Bob Crosbys and the Gray Boys are still winning the battle and old Pres has *got* to be mellow." Taking my hand again, he said, "Let's go somewhere else."

It was late and a yellow harvest moon hung over the isle of Manhattan, where no harvest had been sown for many years. Finding a quiet coffee shop, we sat at an outdoor table, enjoying the clean cold air, and talked.

"I bumped into Herschel's wife last month," I said. "We had a nice talk. She's remarried."

Pres' eyes looked suddenly devastated. "Hersh was my brother. He loved you, too, Lady Ave."

Not meaning to, I shuddered. "He saved my life."

We were quiet for a spell, watching the late night wanderers. The trees cast leafy shadows on the sidewalk.

"Heard about Fort Morrill," he said. "Heard about it the next morning."

I took a sip of my coffee. "News travels quickly."

"Indeed—especially if you're *in* Fort Morrill."

A couple holding hands strolled past. *Only in Greenwich Village*, I thought approvingly—he was white and she was even darker than I.

"What do you mean?" I asked.

Smiling a bitter snaggle-toothed smile, Pres cut out the jive talk. "I mean that I was sitting in a cell in the brig on base the night you were there. It was *killing* me that I couldn't jump up on stage to join you. The guards kept taunting me: *Your friends have probably arrived by now. Oh, they're definitely starting their show by now.* Cruel cats."

"But . . . why?"

Reaching into a side pocket, Pres drew out a silver flask. Winking, he opened it, pouring a generous amount of whiskey into his coffee. "Had a Bob Crosby who was a *bitch*, man. One day he saw a picture of my lady—who, unfortunately, is no longer Pres' lady—on my little table next to my bed. 'You're going with a white woman, *boy*?' he yells in my face. 'No, no, no, sir,' old Pres replies, 'I'm going with your *mother* and man, is she good!'"

Almost choking on my coffee, I sputtered, "You really *said* that?"

Taking a sip of his coffee-flavored whiskey, Pres smiled and nodded.

"What happened then?"

"The bitch punched me out. He punched old Pres in the stomach and then the chops." He opened his mouth wide to show me some obviously missing teeth. "They threw me in the brig all bloody. No doctor came. No food came. No *nothin'* came for a very long time."

My dear friend—one of the greatest artists to ever pick up a saxophone, a musical dreamer who had inspired an entire generation of musicians—looked so beat, so desolate, that I wanted to hug him. So I did. He began to weep.

"They left me alone in that cell for *weeks*, Lady Ave. Weeks. Sometimes I had imaginary conversations with you and Holy

Main and Lady Jo and Lady Jimmy, just to keep sane. But especially with you, Lady Ave."

I hugged my friend even tighter.

And soon we were in my third floor bedroom overlooking Patchen Place.

Fifteen

The next morning Pres was gone. He had left a note on my kitchen table:

Lady Ave:

I always knew you were beautiful—but not this beautiful.

Love you always,

Pres.

P.S. Off to Los Angeles, big eyes for this gig.

Beside the note was a small glass bottle of witch hazel and one cotton ball.

Walking to the laundromat, I felt fine—not sad at all. Buying a *Daily News*, I sat on a plastic chair, read the news, and watched my clothes go round and round. Later in the day I would be at Nola Studios, recording a new song—my first in several years—but for now I was free.

I remember stopping for a coffee to go from a street vendor; it was difficult to carry both my laundry bag and the hot cardboard cup. When I returned to my apartment building, a man—short, balding, white, about my age—saw my predicament and held the front door for me.

"Thank you," I said.

"Can I hold the inner door, too?" he asked in heavily accented

English. My spine stiffened: He sounded German. I must have shot him the evil eye, because he visibly shrank, as if I'd made a move to strike him—which, of course, I hadn't. I was at least two inches taller than he.

"Thank you," I said in my coldest voice.

The recording session that afternoon was a hoot. Basie was on piano with Big 'Un on bass. However, the drummer was Sonny Greer; the alto saxophonist was Johnny Hodges; and the trumpeter was Rex Stewart. All three were Duke Ellington's men and I loved them.

"You're looking fine as wine," said Sonny, a hyper stringbean of a man. "You're *glowing*, girl."

For a second I wondered if Sonny had bumped into Pres, but I kept my cool.

"So are you, Sonny—but I think your glow owes a lot to that whiskey bottle over there."

"Nothing gets past you, Miss Avery Hall," said Sonny approvingly. If you shrank in his presence, you were dead meat—but if you gave it back to him, he admired you for it.

"So, thinking of coming back?" asked Basie, plunking a few notes at the piano.

"*Say, Yes*," mouthed Big 'Un with a wink.

"Not yet, Boss," I said, feeling rather sad at my answer. "I'm enjoying the time off too much. I love sleeping in my own bed." Thinking of Pres, I almost giggled.

"Never join Duke then," said Johnny. "We never stop moving. Off to San Francisco tonight."

The numbers we recorded that day—*Avery's Blues* and *Something Up Ahead*—were minor jukebox hits that you might have heard. I wrote the first one myself (words *and* music) and I'm rather proud of it.

After the session, Sonny, Big 'Un and I enjoyed some barbecue sandwiches at a funky dive, then I took the subway home. I was checking my mail in my building's lobby when that same balding little man appeared. His mailbox was right above mine and he waited patiently.

"Thank you," he said again in his German accent when I stepped aside. Now I have trouble controlling my face; I must have looked evil, because he said, "Have I done something to offend you, Miss?"

"I simply don't like Germans," I replied. "You and your Hitler almost destroyed the world."

Was his smile sad? I'm not sure. But his eyes sure were blue.

"I agree with you. He destroyed mine." Opening his mailbox, he sighed to see it was empty. "As a black lady, you should know better."

It was time to put on my *Avery Sassy Voice*: "Know better than to *what?*"

"Be a bigot," he said, walking out the lobby door.

For a moment I was ready to shrug it off and forget his comment, but something—pigheadedness?—made me dash outside. For a short dude, he sure walked fast.

"Hey, you!" I called. He stopped in front of Renaldi's, the neighborhood green grocers.

"Yes?" he said, those blue eyes boring straight into mine. He was a nervy little guy, I'll give him that.

"I'm no bigot," I said, ready to call down every curse I could on his balding head.

He looked amused. "No?"

"No way."

"Then stop judging me because of my accent. You don't know me." Holding out his hand, he smiled. It lit up his face. "So *get* to know me: My name is Karl Flach. I am a German Jew from Berlin. I arrived in your glorious country two months ago."

Was I ashamed? Yup. For a few moments I had trouble making eye contact.

"My name is Avery—Avery Hall." No reaction. Obviously, he was no jazz fan. "There's a bar up the street, McSweet's. Can I buy you a drink?" I asked.

For the second time I saw Karl's open-hearted smile—the smile that (I later found) revealed all the kindness in his soul. "A lovely lady buying me a drink? This country is even more glorious than I suspected!"

It was a balmy October late afternoon. We sat at a table inside McSweet's and talked for hours. The place went from empty to packed then back to empty, and still we talked. The air smelled of beer and hamburgers grilling. Someone kept playing Charlie Parker's version of *Out of Nowhere* on the jukebox—nickel after nickel after nickel—and it was one of those moments when you think, *Life is perfect.*

"So you arrived two months ago?" He nodded. "Did you arrive from Berlin?"

Sipping his beer, Karl winced. "I hate cold beer. In Germany we drink it at room temperature." He was wearing a raggedy green sweater and pressed gray corduroy trousers. I was beginning to really like his face. "No, I arrived by train from San Francisco. Before that, I arrived in San Francisco on the ocean liner *Marine Lynx* from Shanghai, China."

I almost choked on my wine. "*China?*" I remembered something: "I have a friend named Buck Clayton—he's a famous trumpeter. He lived in Shanghai in the Thirties. Did you ever hear him play there?"

Another wince from the cold beer. "No, no, there was no time for entertainment. When did your friend leave?"

"I'm not sure—I think around 1935."

I was beginning to like his precise German accent. "No, no,

I arrived in Shanghai in July of '39. Your friend was long gone by then."

Outside the window the sunlight was filtering through the orange and yellow leaves. An elderly couple, holding hands, strolled past. The man whispered something in the woman's ear and she laughed.

Karl's face looked as if he'd just been knifed in the stomach.

"What's wrong?" I asked.

He was quiet for a long while. When he looked up, his blue eyes were filled with tears. "I was just thinking of my parents."

Afraid to ask, *Where are they?,* I said nothing.

Finally, he spoke: "It is being estimated that Hitler killed over six million Jews. My parents were two out of that number. Actually, I don't know for certain my father's fate, but in my heart I know he's dead."

In these situations, when one does not know what to say, I've found that two words, said with sincerity, will suffice: "I'm sorry."

Patting my hand, Karl managed a small smile. "It does put a damper on the conversation, doesn't it? Where were we? Ah, yes: your friend, Buck. No, no, he was long gone by the time I arrived."

"Why were you in Shanghai?" I asked.

"Once I escaped from Germany, it was the only place to go. You see, in 1939 Shanghai was still an 'International City.' One did not need a passport or visa to enter. Over twenty thousand Jewish refugees flooded in. I was one of them."

By 1947 the world was hearing of *The Holocaust*—the systematic murders of Jewish men, women, and children carried out by Adolf Hitler and his Nazis. Back in 1939, though, when I was crisscrossing the country with the Count Basie Orchestra, none of us knew what was happening in Germany, or what lay ahead for the Jewish people.

"Were you in a concentration camp?" I asked.

"Yes, for three months. But it is too lovely a day to discuss it."

A few men at the bar, beers in hand, were looking over at our table. Back then it *was* an odd sight: a black woman sitting and speaking with a white man with an accent. This being Greenwich Village, however, we were left alone. Another song was playing on the jukebox: Count Basie's *Blue and Sentimental*, with my Herschel playing like an angel. Now it was my turn to well up.

Touching the back of my hand, Karl said, "What is wrong?"

"Do you hear that saxophone?" Karl nodded. "It's being played by a dear friend of mine who is now gone, too."

He squeezed my hand. "I suppose we both have our stories, don't we?"

"Probably."

"Maybe we should tell them on another day."

Like the gentleman he was, Karl walked me back to our apartment building.

"I enjoyed talking with you, Avery Hall," he said. "I hope we shall do it again."

And with a bow, he was gone.

Sixteen

I didn't see Karl for at least a month. I had decided to dip my toe back into music with several gigs in Newark, Trenton, Atlantic City, and Philadelphia with local, pick-up bands. *Avery's Blues* was released and it was a kick to hear it playing in a bar in the City of Brotherly Love. When I returned to my apartment, there was laundry to do and checks to write, and a steady November rain had begun to strip the leaves from the trees.

One dark rainy evening, around six, someone knocked on my door. It was Karl. He was wearing that green sweater again.

"Good evening, Avery Hall. I was beginning to think that you had moved."

Explaining the gigs, I invited him in, and put the kettle on. We sat at my kitchen table, sipping tea, listening to the wind rattle the windowpanes. It felt good to be warm and indoors. My radio's volume was low, playing classical music. Only one lamp was lit in the living room.

"That's Vivaldi," said Karl, his eyes far away. "My parents loved Vivaldi—and Mozart."

Touching the back of his hand, I said, "I'll listen if you want to talk about it."

Karl was quiet for quite a while. Then looking out the window at the bare, wind-tossed trees, he began to talk:

"It's a long story, one I cannot tell in one night. But I was born in Berlin, my parents' only child. After college, I worked as an accountant at the *Commerz* Bank, which had 53 branches in Berlin alone. Since I did not make much money, I remained at home with my parents. I was the only Jew working at the bank, but before Hitler came to power my religion did not matter to anyone—like what color socks I wore. In fact, I had several very good friends at the bank—all Christian—and every Tuesday evening we would attend an opera together, followed by dinner at a café or restaurant.

"One evening in September 1935, I went out with my friends after work. We saw Verdi's opera *Othello* and afterwards sat at an outdoor café. It was a warm evening so we took our time, sipping wine and beer, talking of the production. One of my Christian friends, a woman, spoke of several rapes in her neighborhood and asked if one of us would walk her home. I volunteered and saw her safely to her apartment door.

"The next morning at work I saw this same woman in the hallway. I said *Hello*. Instead of saying *Hello* back, she covered her eyes, yelled *Jew!*, and ran away. *What did I do?* I asked myself. *Did I tell her a dirty joke last night?* I was baffled. When I walked into our cafeteria, where we all gathered before the bank opened, all of my co-workers, even my friends, stood, gave the Nazi salute, and shouted, *Heil, Hitler!* After that, working at the bank was hell."

"But what changed?" I asked. Karl was still staring out the window.

"The evening before, while we were in the opera house, Hitler had announced his *Nuremberg Laws*, one of which was that German Christians could no longer be friendly to German Jews."

"Sounds like our Jim Crow Laws down South," I said.

"I am not familiar with that term."

I touched the back of his hand. "Another day. Please, continue with your story."

"By 1936 I—and all of Germany's Jews—had been fired from our jobs and confined to the Jewish ghettos of the cities. We had to wear a yellow Star of David—the symbol of our faith—on our blouse, shirt, or jacket. Food was scarce but we bartered with each other in the ghetto. Strangely, one morning a week a box of food—eggs, bread, often some cheese—was left outside my parents' apartment door. I'll never know for sure, but I believe a Christian friend from the bank named Otto was the one leaving this food."

"What makes you think it was him?" I asked.

"Because at the bank my co-workers had been shunning me, and a few even tried to spit in my food at lunchtime. But Otto, if no one else was around, would wink—and I knew that the wink meant: *I'm still your friend, Karl, but what can I do?*

"Then came November 9, 1938, the evening we Jews are beginning to call *Kristallnacht*. Translated, it means *The Night of Shattered Glass*."

Again, Karl was staring out the window. Sheets of wind-driven rain flowed down the glass. His tea was growing cold. "I was out all afternoon, doing various accounting jobs for folks in exchange for food. I was walking back to my parents' apartment when I heard a roar—like a stadium filled with sports fans. I don't recall thinking, just acting—I tore the yellow Star of David off my shirt and threw it in an alleyway. As I approached my block, I could smell smoke. The few remaining Jewish businesses in the ghetto were burning. I saw a mob destroying homes, dragging people from their homes. I saw children being hurt." For a moment Karl had to collect himself. "All I could think to do was to see if my parents were safe."

For the first time since he had begun, Karl looked into my eyes. "When I reached our street, I could see that our apartment building was untouched. But just then I saw a group of Jewish men and boys being marched away. When I gazed too long at them, a Gestapo officer shoved me into the line. It all happened in a terrible moment."

"Were your parents safe?" I asked.

"Yes. They had turned out all the lights in their apartment and were not noticed. Please, Avery, more tea?"

Pouring fresh water into the kettle, I listened as Karl continued: "For the first time in two years I left the Berlin ghetto. We did not know where we were marching to. 'Are they going to shoot us?' I heard a man whisper. '*Silence, Jewdogs!*' screamed one of the Gestapo, hitting that man in the back with his rifle butt. No one whispered after that.

"We marched for at least an hour. It was so cold. On the outskirts of Berlin I saw a train with many cars—*cattle-cars*, they were called. The Gestapo herded us into these cars, which were made of wood. I couldn't believe how tightly they were packing my car. Just when I thought the Nazis could not fit another person into it, they shoved ten more in. Of course, we could not sit. My arms were pinned to my side. Scratching my nose took at least thirty seconds to accomplish. After the door was closed, we heard a padlock, and very soon the train started moving."

"Where were you headed?" I asked.

"We did not know. Since there were no Gestapo in our car, we could speak freely. 'I've heard that they put these cars on a sidetrack, douse them in gasoline, and set them on fire,' one young man said.

"There was no room to sit, no toilets, no food, no water. You must forgive me because this is disgusting, but after many hours we began to do our business in our pants." Another gust of rainy wind shook the windows. "This train ride lasted all day. By nightfall we were beyond hungry, beyond thirsty, beyond filthy. My tongue felt as thick as my arm.

"Finally the train slowed to a crawl, then to a stop. We thought this was it. 'They'll either shoot us now or set the cars on fire,' said a voice. Yet soon after we heard a key in the lock and then the doors opened. '*Welcome to Dachau, Jewdogs,*' said an SS officer in a gleaming black helmet, with death-head skulls on his collar. '*Out!*'"

"I'm sorry," I said, pouring two cups of tea, "but was Dachau a concentration camp?" Today I'm ashamed that I did not know its name.

"Yes, it was Hitler's first, built soon after he came to power. The Nazis' first victims were not the Jews. It's hard to conceive, but the first victims were the people Hitler called *useless eaters.* What a horrible term. They were the people that any compassionate society takes care of—the elderly, the sick, the blind, the mentally slow. Hitler wanted his hospital beds empty and waiting for his Master Race soldiers when the war he envisioned began. The *useless eaters* were taking up space, so they were the first to die at Dachau. Terrible."

"How long were you there?" I asked.

Karl closed his eyes. "From November 10, 1938 to January 25, 1939." *About the time you were first singing with Count Basie*, I thought to myself. "A man said to me once, 'You were only in Dachau for three months?' I replied, 'My friend, considering the hell it was, three *seconds* would have been too long.'"

Outside the windows it was now dark evening. With the rain still falling and my apartment in shadows, it felt like we were the only two souls in the universe. I put my hand over his.

"If this is too painful to talk about, I understand," I said.

Seeming to rouse himself, Karl opened his eyes. "No, no. It's just that I've never told anyone the details of my life. Never. This is the first time I've spoken in depth of those days. I do not wish to bore you."

Oh, you're not boring me, buddy, I thought to myself. "I've read about the camps in *Time* magazine," I said. "What did they look like?"

"Dachau on this first night was a collection of wooden barracks, patrolled by SS officers with police dogs. The camp was of course fenced in, with barbed wire on top of the metal fences, which alone were at least ten feet high. It was a very cold night; we could see our breath. The SS were bundled up snug in their black overcoats, their black helmets, their gleaming black boots. We, however, were stripped naked, hosed down with icy water, and given thin striped uniforms to wear. Any gloves we had were taken away. Luckily, the Nazis allowed us to keep our shoes or boots—for now.

"Our barracks were wooden and unheated. Our beds were slabs of wood with no pillows nor blankets. If you turned too quickly in your sleep, you collected splinters. That first night I curled up into the fetal position, too numb to care, and fell instantly asleep.

"Seemingly a moment later an SS officer was pacing up and down, hammering at a tin pot. '*Time to rise and shine, Jewdogs*,' he said. '*It's another beautiful day in Dachau.*' It was still dark outside. We were each given a hunk of brown bread. Several buckets with ladles were placed on the floor. The water was frozen that first morning so we had to break the ice before drinking. I saw several maggots in my piece of bread. Naturally I scooped them out, throwing them on the floor, before eating.

"'My friend,' said a prisoner who was a doctor, 'there is no protein in bread—but there *is* protein in the maggots. If you wish to survive, do not scoop them out.'"

"You're kidding me," I said.

Karl managed a grin. "They went rather well with red wine."

Noticing that my hand was still on his, I stood up. "Would you like more tea? I can make a sandwich, too—with no maggots in the bread."

"But we need our protein. . . ."

While I made more tea, two tuna fish sandwiches, and a small salad, Karl continued his story. . . .

Seventeen

"When I think back on Dachau, I think of always being cold, always being hungry, always being thirsty. That hunk of bread was our only food until the evening, when we were given another hunk. We were not allowed to wash and we did our business in the wasteland behind the barracks.

"Soon we were standing at attention before the *comman-dant*—the head SS officer. '*Jewdogs*,' he said, '*you are here to work. If you work you may survive. If you cease to work, you will not.*' He then headed inside to an office building with heat steam rising from several chimneys. The remaining SS officers—and there were many, all carrying machine guns—herded us to a corner of the camp where stood a small mountain of boulders. '*You will be carrying these boulders to the other side of the camp*,' said one guard.

"'Why?' asked a teenage boy I knew from the village, a cocky kid. *Boom!* The guard's rifle butt slammed into his mouth, knocking the poor kid to the ground. He was choking on his own teeth. None of us dared help him." Karl looked into my eyes. "The Nazis did not play games."

American racists and Nazis have a lot in common, I thought to myself.

"But why carry boulders?" I asked.

"Simply to torture us. All day into the night we carried them. At midday we were given a bit of water, but no food. My hands were frozen, cut open and bleeding. At times I felt that I was sleepwalking. After at least a decade a guard blew a whistle. '*Jewdogs, go to your barracks.*' I had no idea what time it was, but there were stars in the black sky when we began working and stars in the black sky when we finished. We staggered back to our ice-cold barracks, scarfed down our hunk of bread and maggots, and drank a little water. I crawled into the fetal position and fell instantly asleep.

"Seemingly a second later an SS soldier was banging on a tin pan with a hammer. '*Up, Jewdogs—time for another day at Dachau.*' This second day we were told to move our new mountain of boulders back to its original spot. This time the cocky kid—who was no longer so cocky—did not ask why. Once again, we worked until nightfall, ate our hunk of bread, drank our cup of water, and slept like dead men."

I looked at this man sitting in my apartment, looked at his hands, now healed, which had carried boulders across a concentration camp.

"How did you survive?" I asked.

"I do not know," said Karl, gazing out the window at the skeleton trees in the rain. "Praying helped. Every night I prayed for my mother and father."

"Wait a minute. You still believe in God?"

Karl looked shocked—and hurt. "Of course. My faith saw me through. Don't you?"

I thought for a second before answering. "I don't know. Maybe there's a God, maybe there isn't. I don't know."

Thinking back to that terrible night in Memphis, I recalled the physical pain, the panic, the smell of whiskey on my attacker's breath—and the small cross he wore on a chain around his neck. Believing in God does not guarantee goodness.

"I don't know how someone could live *without* faith in God," said Karl.

"People do it every day. And most of them live good lives. Let's face it—your God could be doing a better job protecting good people from the Nazis of this world." I didn't mean my voice to sound so harsh.

"I'm sorry, Avery," he said. "I did not mean to insult you."

Placing my hand over his, I said, "No, that was harsh. To be honest, I simply don't know."

Karl smiled—a sad smile. "And maybe that's the most honest answer of all." He stood up. "I should be going. I've talked your ears off."

I stood up, too. "No, no. Please don't go. Here, let me put on more water for tea. Please . . . don't go. I'm interested."

He sat down. "Are you sure? It is a relief to finally speak of these things, but I don't wish to drone on and on."

"Hush. Did you ever get a day off from the boulders?" Filling the kettle with water and turning on the burner, I sat down and listened.

"No, it was seven days a week. But days meant nothing in Dachau. Minutes, weeks, months—they meant nothing. We never saw a clock. But one evening—I'm positive it was in December—time suddenly meant everything. Time meant survival.

"I was in a deep sleep when the hammering on the tin pot began. '*Time to get up, Jewdogs!*' cried an SS officer.

"'It can't be morning already,' I murmured, almost to myself.

"'Karl,' said Heinz, the man in the bunk beneath me, 'I haven't yet fallen asleep. It is the same night.'

"I was almost hoping that the Nazis were going to execute us—to put me out of this ceaseless hunger and cold. Having no choice, I followed my fellow prisoners out into the night. It was bitterly cold, with about an inch of icy snow on the ground. Our striped uniforms gave us no warmth, but the SS officers looked warm as toast in their black overcoats and mufflers and gloves. The commandant was out, too, grinning like a sweepstakes winner.

"I'll never forget the stars that night: They were so clear, so close, so uncaring about our problems. And believe me, we had problems, because the commandant cleared his throat and said, '*Jewdogs, we have a little game here tonight at Dachau. Remove your hats.*' Since our hats gave us little warmth, that was no loss. '*Now remove your shoes, your boots, your socks.*' We could not believe our ears, but machine guns were pointed at us."

"My God," I said, "and there was snow on the ground."

Karl nodded. "Crusty, icy snow. Within fifteen seconds you were in agony—like icy needles were stabbing the bottoms of your feet. Taking out his pocket watch, the commandant opened it, and said, '*It is now eight-thirty in the evening. You will be standing here until eight thirty* in *the morning. Whoever survives wins the game. Enjoy yourselves.*' And so began the longest night of my life."

I looked at this man—this rather small man—sitting at my kitchen table. *This man's body suffered this ordeal*, I thought to myself.

Karl shuddered. "I often dream of that night, as if it is still happening. The bottoms of my feet soon grew numb. Many times I fell asleep while standing. But then I would awaken, aware of the cold, the pain. After a few hours the older prisoners began to fall in the snow. The Nazis left them alone—they would soon freeze to death."

"Was that the point?"

"Yes. This was 1938. The mass gassings with Zyklon B had

not yet begun. This was one way to have fewer mouths to feed in the morning." Karl snorted. "Our maggoty bread must have cost so much.

"At one point—it must have been two or three in the morning—a young man simply could not take it anymore. Screaming, he ran from the ranks towards the camp's fence. I could not believe my eyes. No Nazi fired at him. *Is it this easy?* I thought. *Simply run away?* But of course it wasn't." He sighed. "The Nazis had had us working in a different part of the camp for the past several days. When the boy dove onto the fence, sparks shot out of his hair. He was wrenched horribly, back and forth, back and forth. The Nazis had . . . what would the word be? *electrocuted*? *electrified*? the fence." Karl's eyes were closed as he remembered. "The boy's father was there to watch as the Nazis laughed. The next morning they brought us over: the boy's face and the palms of his hands were melted into the wire of the fence. They left him there for weeks as a warning—and as a meal for the crows."

Suddenly I began to cry. The memory of being attacked in Memphis replayed in my mind, mingling with the image of the dead Jewish boy. Leaving his chair, Karl knelt in front of me, and held me. Another gust of wind shook my kitchen windows.

"I'm sorry," he said. "My story has upset you."

Collecting myself, I tried to smile. "I just don't understand evil people. Never have. Is it that hard to be kind?"

Returning to his chair, Karl sipped at his cold tea. "For some, yes. But I believe that for most people—no, it is not hard. Most of us are kind. I have to believe that." We were silent for several moments. "Should I go?"

I could barely see his face. It was almost eight o'clock. "No, I want to hear about the rest of the night."

Karl stared out the window. "Well, as the hours passed, many older men and some boys began to fall to the ground. It was mainly the elderly. The S.S. just laughed as these poor souls froze to death before them. I had it easy—my father was not there. I saw young men weeping that night as they watched their fathers or grandfathers or both die in front of their eyes. The S.S. mocked their tears.

"I must have fallen asleep again on my feet because suddenly it was light and the commandant was looking at his watch, saying, '*Congratulations, Jewdogs, you are the ones who have won the game. Go to your barracks.*' The ground was littered with the bodies of the frozen dead. I did not count how many. I was too stunned. I was sitting on my bunk, dead numb, when a kitchen knife was tossed in by a guard. I can still hear it clattering on the wooden floor. '*You may use this to cut the frozen flesh off your feet,*' he said. '*You will be back to work in half an hour.*'"

"You're kidding me," I said. "After working all day, then standing outdoors all night, they made you *work*?"

He nodded. "Yes. Our first task was to drag the bodies of the dead to a ditch and throw them in. Many boys were dragging their father's bodies."

My face must have shown it—I had heard all I could stand. Karl felt it, too. "It is late," he said, standing up, "and I've told my cheerful tale long enough." I was about to protest, but he put a finger to my lips. "No need to disagree. I understand."

As he left my apartment, he turned and said, "Thank you, Avery, for the tea and companionship."

I was left alone.

For the very first time in my life, I was halfway in love.

Eighteen

I didn't see Karl for over a week. A few gigs with pick-up groups in Hoboken and Baltimore and Washington, D.C. brought in some loot. The local musicians weren't much—I'd worked with caviar and champagne musicians with Basie—but I remembered something Ben Webster once said: "If the rhythm section ain't makin' it, Avery, go for yourself." So I did. *Avery's Blues* was doing quite well in Baltimore, so I had to sing it twice each night. Didn't mind, though.

When I woke up one morning in my own bed, for a moment I didn't realize where I was. Cold sunlight was streaming in the windows—it was early December—so I bundled up and headed outdoors.

A few hours later—after breakfast in a diner and many pleasant meanderings—I found myself on a bench in Battery Park, watching the waves spilling over onto the pavement. The sky was ice-blue and the wind off the choppy water was, as Imaginary Father would've said, as "cold as a witch's teat." The Liberty Island ferry had just chugged off when a familiar voice said: "Excuse me, miss, but are you lost?" I turned, and it was Karl. His blue eyes were teary in the brisk wind and his cheeks were red.

I gave him a hug. "What are you doing down here? We're a

long way from the Village."

Brushing off someone's cigarette ash, he sat down beside me. "I like to wander and daydream. This city is as wonderful as Berlin for doing both."

We sat together, chatting about this and that, watching the barges and the ferries and at least one ocean liner heading out past the Narrows. Gulls were gliding over the white-capped waves. "I hope their brains are large enough to realize the fun they're having," said Karl.

An elderly Chinese couple walked past. It sounded as if they were arguing. The husband, walking several steps behind his wife, was doing most of the talking.

Leaning over, Karl said, "He's telling her that he's tired of dumplings. 'Dumplings for breakfast, dumplings for dinner, dumplings, dumplings, dumplings.' She's saying that he can do his own cooking then."

"*You understand Chinese*?" I asked.

His eyes moist from the breeze, Karl nodded. "I lived in Shanghai for eight years. I told you that."

I'd forgotten. Punching him (gently) on the shoulder, I said, "You get around, man."

"Do all American women punch like you?"

"Only a few of us."

"Well, stop, please. You have bony knuckles. Yes, I lived in Shanghai. Back in '39 it was practically the only place on Earth that allowed a Jew to enter without a passport."

"How did you get from Dachau to China?"

He smiled. "You don't mind another tale?"

"No, of course not."

"One moment then." Karl walked over to a nearby vendor and bought two cups of steaming coffee. "Here, something to sip on while I gab on. Where did I leave off last time?"

"That terrible night when you stood outside."

"Oh, yes. Well, that was December 1938. In late January '39 we were standing outside one morning at roll call. My name and number were called. When I raised my hand, an SS officer told me to report to the commandant's office. I thought to myself, 'This is it. You will be dead in a few minutes and free from this place.' We'd all seen the commandant—a true sadist—occasionally shooting people from his office balcony." Wincing, Karl sipped his coffee. "The way a hunter shoots ducks. Twice I was carrying my boulders, aching in every bone, when the man next to me fell with a bullet in the back of his head. You don't know how many times I prayed for its cousin to burrow into my head—and now I was going to the commandant's office. With my eyes I said my goodbyes to my comrades in pain.

"No one escorted me. Although I had never been inside the administration building, I knew the way. As I entered, I received one of the biggest shocks of my life: It was carpeted; it was warm; I could smell coffee; I could hear music from a radio. It was so *normal*—like a bank or an insurance company. I could hear typewriters clacking away. I was shocked to see women—well dressed, warm women—sitting at their desks, doing the clerical work of a concentration camp." Karl shook his head. "Can you imagine? '*Come work for the Fatherland. Good benefits. Keep careful records of how many Jews we kill.*'

"A woman pointed the way to the commandant's office and I knocked on his door. '*Come in,*' he said. I was strangely calm as I turned the door handle. The commandant, with his head down, was doing paperwork. I saluted, recited my number, and said, 'Reporting, Sir. *Heil, Hitler.*' Silence. He kept on scribbling. A folded newspaper was on the corner of his desk. I could read the date: *January 25, 1939*, the day of my death. I knew that in a moment he would open his desk drawer, pull out a pistol, and shoot me in the face. I was ready. The seconds ticked past. Then sighing, he put down his pencil and opened the desk drawer. Closing my eyes, I was ready to hear the last sound I would ever hear—when, *whack!*—I heard paper slapping against wood. Opening my eyes, I saw what looked like a train ticket. I also saw the commandant's face, which was looking at me as if I were not human, as if I were vermin.

"'Take this train ticket. You may leave,' he said.

"'But . . . but . . . how? *Why?*' I asked.

"I'll never forget his icy eyes—they were light blue. 'Stop asking questions before I change my mind.'

"Miraculously, the ticket was still there. It had not vanished. Now I honestly thought that I was dreaming, that this was all fantasy, but I figured, '*What the heck? Ride this pleasant dream as long as you can.*' So I picked up the ticket, saluted, said my *Heil, Hitler* again, and walked out of the office.

"Two guards were waiting for me. Each taking an arm, they escorted me out of the building toward Dachau's locked main gates. In my memories I can't recall ever seeing the sun in Dachau, but I must have. Gray clouds could not have lingered for three months. This morning the sky was like slate and an icy rain had begun. Unlocking the gates, one of the guards shoved me through, then locked them again. I was outside Dachau and the SS were inside. Again, absolutely convinced I was dreaming, I asked, 'Where is the nearest train station?'

"The other guard pointed with his rifle and said, 'Keep going straight for about five miles. You can't miss it, Jewdog.' They turned and walked away.

"I was alone. I remember seeing two black crows on a branch high above, laughing down at me. They also knew I was dreaming. I thought, 'This dream is so wonderful, let's keep it going,' so I walked and walked. Sure enough, I came to a small train station."

A ferry from Liberty Island bumped against the dock. People—mostly couples with children—stepped off the ferry, while people—mostly couples with children—stepped on. For the briefest of seconds, I pictured Karl and myself with beautiful children. The thought shocked me.

"You have to understand, Avery, that I was absolutely *convinced* that I was dreaming. So I stepped onto the train—still in my camp uniform, dirty, stinking. Luckily, the train was not crowded so I sat in a corner by myself. The few passengers stared at me. I gazed out the window, dreading the moment when I would wake up—maybe on my wooden bunk, shivering, or maybe sleeping on my feet, carrying a boulder. But the dream continued.

"In a few hours the train stopped in the Berlin station. I couldn't believe how realistic my dream was—newspaper headlines from a vendor's shop—it was still January 25, 1939—the stares from so many faces, even my own stink. Absolutely vivid.

"Like a sleepwalker, I stumbled through the streets to the Jewish ghetto, walked to my parents' building, climbed the stairs, knocked, and waited. When my dear mother answered the door, wearing an apron over her housecoat, she wailed and grabbed me so hard. 'My baby,' she said over and over, 'my baby.' Thank God it was no dream."

"But why were you released?" I asked. With a chug of smoke, the ferry was headed back to the island. The wintry breeze smelled of diesel and roasting chestnuts.

"I didn't find that out until a few hours later, when my father returned. In the meantime, I had taken three baths. This is quite disgusting but the first bath's water was black, so I emptied the tub, cleaned it, and ran a second bath. The second bath's water was brownish, so I did the same. Only after the third bath was the water—and my body—clean.

"So wrapped in pajamas and a bathrobe, I sat at my mother's kitchen table, sipping tea and eating a bit of toast. My stomach could not handle anything richer. It was close to four in the afternoon and the streetlights outside the apartment were on. I felt like I'd gone from hell to heaven in less than half a day.

"When my dear father returned, we embraced. Both my parents were weeping. We sat in my father's study, with the fireplace roaring, and he told me this story: 'Karl, back in the war I had a friend, whom you've never met, who is now a Nazi official. It took a while, but I was able to track him down. As soon as Hitler came to power, I withdrew all our money and hid it in our mattress. My old friend and I arranged to meet on the edge of the ghetto. Handing him most of the money in an envelope, I asked him to do what he could to spring you from Dachau. A tiny bit of the money was for your train ticket. It took a while, but he kept his word to me. But . . . I did not give him *all* of our money. I kept a bit and was able to buy you a ship's ticket out of this God-forsaken country. Your ship leaves in June.'

"'Am I going to America?' I asked him. Everyone wanted to come to this country. Look out there at your Lady Liberty."

I did—the green lady with the strong right arm was still standing on her island. The ferry was close to docking.

"'No, Karl,' my father said. 'I tried—but it was impossible. No, in June you will be sailing to . . . Shanghai, China.' I was shocked, and he explained how one did not need a passport to enter. Do you realize that there were over twenty thousand Jews living in Shanghai?"

"Yes," I said. "A dear friend once told me."

"Thank you. So that was how I escaped from Dachau."

"Did your parents leave Germany, too?" I asked.

An old lady walking her dog strolled past. She gave us a look, but Karl did not notice. "No. Between bribing me out of Dachau and the boat ticket, all of my parents' money was used up. 'But they'll never hurt me, Karl,' said my father. 'You know I fought for this country in the Great War. I was even decorated for bravery. They won't dare harm me.'"

"Did they?"

Karl sighed. "I don't know for sure. I received my last letter from my father in October 1939. Then the letters stopped. I've been writing monthly letters to the new German government asking about his fate for over a year now. So far, no answer."

When the sun dove behind a bank of purplish clouds, the temperature must have fallen five degrees in a minute. "Want to find a coffee shop?" I asked, and we did, on lower Broadway. Sipping our coffee and sharing a piece of blueberry pie, we continued our talk. A few customers glared at us—a white man sitting with a black woman—but no one said anything.

"What about your mother?" I asked.

My question made Karl wince. "In a moment. So I'm home and it's late January, but I'll be leaving for China on June 13. I have no job and no way of getting one."

"What did you do to pass the time?" I asked.

"First off, I had to report to the local Nazi office on the edge of the ghetto every morning at eight o'clock sharp. I'd be outside a clerk's office, watching the second hand on the clock on the wall. At exactly eight o'clock I would knock. 'Come in.' I'd enter, give the Nazi salute, announce my name, and salute again. The clerk would make a mark in a small book and I'd leave. I did this every morning, seven days a week."

My coffee felt and tasted delicious. "What if you slept late—or forgot?"

"I would have been tossed back into Dachau. The rest of the day, I took walks—often with my father—and I visited friends in the ghetto. You see, we were not permitted to leave the Jewish ghetto. But the time weighed on us. My mother was a rather nervous woman, and she broke down crying quite often. The shadow of our parting always hung over us.

"Soon enough, the evening of June 12 arrived: The next morning my ship would be leaving from Bremerhaven—a seaside town. My mother had to excuse herself from the dinner table and we could hear her weeping in her bedroom.

"Around seven in the evening there was a vicious knocking on the apartment door. My father answered: It was two Gestapo soldiers. 'We are here to watch your son pack,' they announced."

"You're kidding," I said.

"Do you doubt the Nazis' efficiency?" asked Karl. "They were as organized as . . . as Nazis. No, anyone leaving Germany could only bring ten marks—about sixty dollars—out of the country. So I'm on my hands and knees in my bedroom, packing my suitcase, with two Gestapo watching me. About my age, they began chatting away with each other. Figuring they wouldn't shoot me in my own bedroom, I found the courage to ask, 'Excuse me, can I bring this camera?' It was my Nikon; I still own it.

"One of them grabbed it, opening the back to see if there was any money hidden—ruining a good roll of film, I might add. 'Fine—take your camera—*but nothing else!*' When I was packed—two changes of clothes, shaving gear, a new toothbrush—they whipped out a roll of thick tape decorated with swastikas and taped my suitcase over and over and over. The handle was even buried under many layers of tape. Then they left."

Karl had stopped looking at me and was instead gazing out the coffee shop window. Since we were close to the Fulton Fish Market, many trucks roared past.

"The next morning my father and I ate a silent breakfast. We could hear my mother wailing in her bed."

Just then an old white biddy, leaving the shop, muttered something under her breath that sounded like, "Shocking." I was about to make a nasty reply, but a gentle look from Karl stopped me. Funny—but I didn't think of Karl as *white*. I simply thought of him as Karl.

"What's the point?" he said after the witch had left. "She doesn't understand life—and probably never will. As I said, my mother was crying so hard. It frightened me. 'You have to go in to say goodbye, Karl,' my father said. We were ready to leave for the train station. When I knelt by her bed, she grabbed me around the neck and wouldn't let go. '*My baby, my baby, my baby*,' she kept crying. I was weeping, too, but it was uncomfortable—my neck began to ache. She literally would not let me go. Finally, my father gently untangled her fingers, saying, '*Shh*, Rosa—Karl must leave. It is time.' As my father and I left our apartment and walked down the staircase, I could hear my mother's wailing growing fainter and fainter."

Karl was silent. Someone had put a nickel in the jukebox; Billie Holiday began to sing *Lover Man*. "More coffee?" asked the waitress, a black girl. I nodded for both of us.

"You know, I haven't spoken of this to anyone," said Karl, placing his hand over mine. "This is the first time I've ever said these things aloud."

"You can stop."

"Do you wish me to? Am I boring you?"

"No—stop asking me that. I just mean if it's too painful. This is the least boring story I've ever heard." And I meant it.

"Alright then. This coffee, by the way, is very good." He looked out the window at the ceaseless traffic. "At the train station my father embraced me. Both of us were doing our best not to cry. 'I love you, son,' he said, and I told him the same. My seat in the train faced the tracks so I opened the window and waved until he was just a speck, then no more. That was the last time I ever saw my parents."

"Do you think they're dead?" I asked, regretting instantly how cold my question sounded. I thought of my own mother.

"My mother, yes—she is dead. As I told you, I'm not sure about my father. But in my heart I believe he, too, is gone.

"At Bremerhaven I found the ship my father had secured for me—the *Gneisenau*, it was called. Because he bought a first class ticket, my cabin was superb. Never having been to sea before, I was much too excited to sleep. So near midnight I stood at the railing, watching the water churn past. Since it was very chilly I'd worn a jacket, and when I put my hands in the pockets, I felt something—my mother's wedding ring." Reaching beneath his shirt, he pulled out a necklace, with the ring attached. "I don't know if my mother put it in my pocket when she was hugging me—or if it was my father at the train station. Either way, I wear it everywhere."

"Excuse me." It was the black waitress, looking embarrassed. "The manager says you've been here long enough. Would you mind paying and leaving?"

I was ready to throw a fit, but Karl patted my hand. "No problem, Miss."

"If this were my place, you could stay all day," she said.

"I understand."

Paying for our coffees, Karl smiled at me. "Want to share a taxi back to the Village?"

"Sure, but the taxi's on me."

Back on Patchen Place, we stood in front of our building. A bitter winter's night was about to descend.

"If you're not ready to float away from all that coffee," said Karl, "can I brew you some tea?"

"Sure." Telling me his apartment number, he dashed up the stairs. I stopped off in my place to freshen up.

Karl's apartment, two floors above mine, was Spartan and spotless. His record collection was purely opera, and one I came to love—Mozart's *The Magic Flute*—was playing. After putting the kettle on the stove, he invited me to sit on his couch, which clearly had come from a second hand shop. On the wall was a framed poster of the first Joe Louis-Max Schmeling fight.

"Hey, I was at the second fight!" I said, filling him in on the sad tale of Count Basie's hat.

"Yes, Max didn't last long at that one. I've read about it."

"Why do you have a poster up of that Nazi?" I asked.

"Max Schmeling—a Nazi?" The kettle was screeching and Karl poured our tea. "No, no—he did his best to avoid the Nazis. Of course, he didn't wish to die in a camp either, but Max was not a Nazi. In fact, he hid two Jewish boys during *Kristallnacht*." He looked in pain. "The murders that occurred that night will never be truly counted."

The words were out before I could stop them: "My mother was murdered." I told him everything. Karl's blue eyes listened with such care, such concern, that I was falling more deeply in love by the second with this short, balding, beautiful man.

"So we have both known pain," he said.

"Doesn't everyone?"

"True—but not like ours."

And before I knew it, we were kissing and hugging and kissing some more.

And before I knew it, it was morning.

Nineteen

It was never discussed—we were simply now a couple. Karl never discussed that I was black; I never discussed that he was white. We were each other's dearest friend, we loved each other, and that (to us) was that.

But even though we lived in Greenwich Village—quite possibly the most open-minded neighborhood in America—it was still 1947 and we were still an interracial couple.

But all that was outside the walls of Karl's apartment as we ate scrambled eggs and toast and drank coffee and slept in all that delicious December day.

I found that he was looking for work as an accountant, but so far with no luck. He had quite a bit of money squirreled away but "a job would still be welcome." I told him that I, too, had some blessed loot in the bank and could pick and choose my gigs at will.

"You'll have to come hear me sing sometime," I said, wrapped up in his green bathrobe, sitting on his second-hand couch. Mozart was playing again, very softly.

"I'd love you—I mean *to*. More eggs?" he asked.

"No, come sit down. Tell me about your journey to China."

For the first time all the love songs I'd ever sung made sense. Before—thinking of my poor mother and her host of wretches—those songs had seemed phony and dishonest. No longer.

"Where did I leave off?"

"On the slow boat to China. You had just found your mother's ring."

"Oh, that's right. Well, the journey took six weeks."

"Were you mistreated for being Jewish?"

"No—my first class cabin seemed to shield me from bigotry. Plus, the ship was filled with people from many countries. It also made several stops. I, my dear, have strolled around the Rock of Gibraltar. Another day I explored a seaside village in India whose name I never learned. I saw a snake charmer tease a serpent from a basket with his music. Finally, in late July the *Gneisenau* pulled into Shanghai Harbor.

"I remember staring at the railing, looking down at the unbelievable activity on the docks. People were cooking their meals over car and truck engines. Rickshaws were being pulled in all directions. It was crazy—and I'm looking out, realizing that I don't know one soul in the *entire country*, that I don't speak the language, and that ten German marks stand between me and starvation. Finally, grabbing my suitcase (with the swastika tape long torn away), I stepped down the gangplank into Shanghai. *Boom!* I had to dodge a man on a bicycle, who screamed something at me. The crowd was turning me in circles. Suddenly I felt a hard tap on my shoulder. 'Are you Jewish?' asked a man about my own age."

"Wait a minute," I interrupted. "How old are you?"

Karl had been stroking my hair. "I was born in 1911. I'm thirty six. How old are you?"

"I was born in 1919. I'm twenty eight."

He kissed me. "Ah, a younger woman."

I kissed him right back. "Ah, an older man."

I snuggled into his arms as he continued: "Of course, I said, 'Yes, I'm Jewish' and he said, 'Follow me,' rushing into the crowd. Now I had a decision to make: Was this fellow honest—or was he going to rob me in an alley? Shanghai has quite the reputation for its crime, you know. Anyways, I decided to follow the man, and I had to hustle to keep up as he darted down alleys and through narrow streets. Finally, we stood in front of a tall brick factory building. 'Here is your new home,' he announced."

"I don't understand," I said.

"I didn't either, until the fellow explained: 'The Jewish Philanthropic Society has purchased this building. You may stay as long as you like. You will receive one free ladle of soup in the morning and one in the evening. Your other meals are up to you.' He then dashed off to help other new arrivals. Inside it was chaos—no beds, but bamboo mats on the floor to show where people slept. Another man showed me to my spot on the third floor and I put down my suitcase. 'You will sleep on this mat,' he said. 'Towels are in the shower room. Breakfast is served at six. You are also allowed endless writing paper, envelopes and postage. Watch your back on the streets.'

"So I unpacked, took a cold shower, dressed in fresh clothes, and went for my first Shanghai walk. I made a vow not to spend one *penny* of my money, but to live off the morning soup ration. With all the delicious smells of good food cooking *everywhere* it was nearly impossible to keep my vow—but I did. That night I wrote a letter to my parents, instructing them to write back to me care of *The Jewish Philanthropic Society, Tangshaw Road, Shanghai, China*. My bamboo mat was not terribly comfortable—but it was (compared to Dachau) not terribly uncomfortable either—and it was free. I had a home in my new country."

My eyes were closed as I tried to picture Shanghai. "What was it like?"

"People everywhere—rickshaws everywhere—busy everywhere. Big pots of food cooking right out in the open. Outdoor barbershops with men being shaved. It was also a relief, after the Berlin ghetto, to be outside and walking without fences, without Gestapo. My stomach was always empty—two ladles of soup a day do not satisfy—but I was too excited, too curious to stop walking.

"Because Shanghai is in the tropics, it is beastly hot. One morning when I saw a clean straw hat on top of a garbage can, I took it. Here I am, strolling along, proud of my new hat, when a hand reached out from a rickshaw and grabbed it off my head! The rider yelled something to the driver—it must have been the Chinese version of *giddyup*!—because the rickshaw, and my new hat, were soon out of sight.

"One day a similar thing happened with my pipe. A hand reached out of a bus window and yanked the pipe right out of my mouth. I almost lost my teeth! It was a good way to stop smoking, I'll tell you that."

Something occurred to me: "You speak English so well, Karl. Where did you learn?"

"In school in Berlin. I read most of Charles Dickens' novels—in English. Plus, before Hitler, American movies were always being shown in the cinema. I learned *giddyup* from *Hopalong Cassidy* films. It made communicating in Shanghai much easier because I found that many people spoke English. The letters I wrote to my parents, though, were always in German. By late August the first letters from my father began to arrive. I still have them; I'll show them to you someday. They were all neatly typed, but he signed them, in aqua ink, *Love, Pa and Ma.* These letters were filled with local news, but because he knew the Nazis were reading our mail, he never mentioned anyone's name. He always told me how much he and my mother missed me. At one point I was writing my parents two letters a day—one in the morning and one in the evening—and I was receiving almost daily letters from my father. Then in October his letters stopped—I don't know for certain why—but I'll always remember his last one." Karl closed his eyes, reciting from memory: "*Dear Son, please forgive me. I have been lying to you.*"

"Why?" I interrupted. "What was the lie?"

Karl was looking out the window. It was snowing. "The lie was signing the letters, *Pa and Ma.* My father wrote, '*Your dear mother did not wake up the morning after your boat left Germany.*' The poor man knew I had enough to deal with, getting used to my new home. For a while he wanted to spare me the pain." We were both quiet. "And that was the last letter I received from him. On the first of every month I mail another letter to the new German government, asking of my father's fate, but so far without a reply."

"What do you think your mother died of?" I asked—wishing right away that I hadn't.

"She was not sick, at least not physically, so. . . ."

Pres was the only other person I had ever held, the only other person I had ever comforted. It was as though Karl and I were the only two people in the world. I loved this man.

A few hours later I had just stepped out of the shower in my apartment when the phone rang.

"Avery?" It was Basie; he was surrounded by noise.

"Boss? It's me."

"I can barely hear you. Buck and I are at the Onyx on 52nd Street digging Bird. Come on up!"

"Can I bring a friend?" I asked.

"Bring a thousand friends! The Onyx. *Now!*"

Karl picked up his phone on the third ring. "Hello?"

"Want to come with me to a jazz club on 52nd Street? Count Basie will be there and Charlie Parker is playing."

"I've heard of Basie, of course, but not the other fellow. I'll be down in a minute."

The white cabbie kept shooting us strange looks in his rear view mirror. I was all ready for combat when he said, "You used to sing with Basie, right?"

"Yeah," I said. "My name's Avery Hall."

"That's right, that's right. Saw you guys in Newark back before the war. Man, that band could *swing*."

A line of people stood outside the Onyx, waiting for the next set—and there stood Buck, who hustled us past the crowd and down the stairs. I didn't even have time to introduce him to Karl, and it was too loud and frantic in the club. Bird and his quintet were eyes-closed *intense*. Basie sat at a corner table, saving three seats.

"Dig *him!*" Basie yelled in my ear. Karl shook hands with my two friends and then settled in for a listen. Man, Bird was *flying*. In a rumpled suit, his tie loosened, he played the blues: Kansas City soul mixed with New York City grit. This was different music from Basie's—not as fleshed out, not as dancer friendly—but it was still beautiful and it swung. Buck's face glowed when Bird's young trumpeter, Miles Davis, played a particularly tricky solo. "The kid's *bad*," he said with a smile. Seeing Karl's perplexed look, I whispered in his ear, "That means he's very, very *good*."

I bought my boyfriend a beer—it was warm, the way he liked it—and we listened for a magical hour to Bird, Miles, Duke Jordan on piano; Tommy Potter on bass; and Max Roach on drums. When the set was over, the others scrambled, but Bird ambled over. With a golden front tooth, he was smooth and charming.

"Man, Basie and Buck! As a kid I used to be in the alley outside the Reno Club, listening to you cats just *wailing*. I remember the night you cats worked up *Blue Balls*."

Basie seemed embarrassed for me. "It's now called *One O'Clock Jump*," he said to Karl. "At the Reno we just started playing those head riffs—from D Flat then on up to F. The thing just stuck. When you gonna come play for me, Bird?"

"Oh, one of these days, Count, one of these days. I was wondering, though." Bird's eyes darted about. "How about an advance on my future earnings?"

Although Basie was grinning, his eyes were diamond hard. "Oh, not tonight, Bird—but after your first gig with my band, you'll get your loot, no worries."

Not long after, as we sat in a booth in a crowded joint on Seventh Avenue, Basie explained: "Bird's a junkie—on heroin. He hits up everyone for money."

"He asked me for some in the men's room," said Karl.

"Did you give him any?" asked Buck.

"No—I could see the needle in his jacket pocket. I saw many addicts in Shanghai."

I thought Buck's eyes were going to explode out of his head. "You've been to *Shanghai*, man?"

"I lived there for eight years," said Karl—and the two were off and running, swapping Shanghai stories, right away fast friends.

"So, how have you been?" asked Basie, putting his big warm hand on mine.

"Fine." I must have smiled like a fourteen year old girl. "I have a boyfriend."

"So I see." Basie looked worried. "Nice guy—but do you know what you two are in for?"

"Nothing's happened yet."

"But it will."

"Maybe." I laughed. "Maybe we can find a blind rabbi to marry us."

Those big Basie eyes bore into mine. "Just be careful, Ave. Watch your fine behind." Changing the subject, he asked, "You ready to go back on the road yet? There's always a job waiting. Got a girl singer with us now, but she's not you."

I kissed the dear man's cheek. "Not yet—but I appreciate the offer."

In the cab downtown, Karl raved about Buck. "And he's a musician, too, you say?"

"One of the finest trumpeters in jazz. He's famous."

"Well, he and I are meeting for breakfast tomorrow. He said he'd like to see my Shanghai photographs."

"I'd like to see them, too."

"You, my love, don't have to wait for breakfast."

Back in his apartment, Karl carefully spread the photographs on his kitchen table. All in black-and-white, they were shots of the streets, of people's faces, of an outdoor barber shop, of the Shanghai docks. "I love them all," I said, "but this is my favorite. You can tell that in a *second* that man on the left is going to take his next step, and the rickshaws are going to speed past."

"Photography is time frozen," said Karl. "Photography is frozen time."

"Not bad," I said. "But where did you get the money for film? Did you spend the ten marks?"

While brewing tea, Karl continued his story: "One day it was announced that all Jewish refugees—who were still flooding into Shanghai—had to have photo IDs. The local Chinese photographers were charging the equivalent of ten dollars per photo. One afternoon, on one of my wandering walks, I saw an empty storefront, with a stool someone had left behind. Then I saw an old but clean blanket in a trash can. Finding some wire, I hung the blanket at the sidewalk end of the storefront. Then I broke down and went to a printer. ***JEWISH PHOTOGRAPHER, FIVE DOLLARS PER PHOTO***, the posters read, and I included the address of the storefront. Buying some film and borrowing a bicycle from a friend, I pedaled all over the city, hanging my posters. Within several days the lines stretched around the block. Who wouldn't prefer a photo for half the price? Each and every person clutched an American five dollar bill and I no longer had to survive on two ladles of soup a day."

"You're a hustler, my friend."

Karl's blue eyes shone. "Oh, you have no idea. The fanciest restaurant in Shanghai is called the *Sun-Sun*. I went to the owner, Mr. Lee, and offered my services as the restaurant's photographer. I would stroll through the restaurant, which was always crowded, and ask people if they wished for a souvenir photograph. I didn't charge much and I split the fee with Mr. Lee—but so many customers wanted their picture taken that even more money was flowing in. So during the day I conducted my photo ID business and at night I ate for free at the *Sun-Sun*." He pointed at another photo. "Now this one was taken in the Chinese district of Shanghai, where Westerners were not

allowed. Those men are all thinking, 'What is that Westerner doing here?' But Mr. Lee gave me a pass that allowed me to go into that part of the city." Karl's eyes shone. "What a rare gift that was."

During our talks, Karl would ask about my life. Bit by bit, I told him about my childhood with my mother and her parade of boyfriends, about my life on the road with Basie, and about Memphis. "You were lucky that your friend Herschel was nearby," he said. "I should like to meet him."

"He died back in '39," I said, and from out of nowhere I began to cry. Folding me in his arms, Karl held me tightly. "We've both lost people we've loved," he said. "Maybe that's why we belong together."

The next morning he talked our landlady into letting us both out of our leases. A huge loft apartment was empty on the top floor of the building, with a clear view of the Empire State Building from our living room. Like excited kids, we moved in together.

A month later, when we discovered that I was pregnant, we found a color blind justice of the peace and were married . Buck was Karl's best man, and Basie—my Non-Imaginary Father—gave me away.

"Just watch yourselves, you two," said Basie.

Twenty

Two weeks after our marriage, Karl found a job as an accountant at the Werner & Schiff agency. Each morning now—resplendent in one of his three new suits—he left the apartment for the subway ride uptown.

Pres was back in town and we met for lunch at the White Horse Tavern.

"You sure that baby isn't mine?" he asked, his snaggle-toothed grin dialed up to wicked.

"Shut up," I said, laughing in spite of myself. "And I'd appreciate it if you don't share anything with Karl."

"Your knowledge is sacred with me, Lady Ave. Buck, by the way, says that he's a prince—Prince Hubby. So, you been singing?"

"A few gigs here and there. I was always careful with my money, so I can be choosey. How about you?"

Sipping at a small shot glass of whiskey, Pres smiled. "Just recorded with Nat Cole in the City of Angels. Right now Papa Jo and I have a little combo on 52nd Street at the Three Deuces. Bring Prince Hubby and have a ball."

Something about Pres—something rather lost—always made me feel maternal. I put my hand on top of his. "Any lady in your life?"

When we discussed personal matters, Pres' eyes always found something fascinating on the ceiling. "Nah, too busy. Pres is always on the blessed road, chasing the dream. A few lady friends here and there, but not love."

"Funny—I always thought you and Lady Day. . . ."

"Just friends—lifelong friends. She'd rip my little heart in two."

After lunch, Pres walked me to my building. "Want to come up and see our home?" I asked.

"Nah, I've got a date with a lady friend uptown." He kissed me on the cheek, then whistled for a cab. "But Pres wants to see you and Prince Hubby at the Three Deuces. Dig?"

I did. Although my heart could break for my lonely friend, he still made me smile. "Dig, Pres."

And once again, he was gone.

The Three Deuces was packed, with Jo chewing gum and smiling, whisking his drums with brushes. I didn't know the pianist and bass player, but they were solid. Yet it was Pres and Jo the people came to hear. "Just some *chicki-boom, chicki-boom*, Lady Jo," said Pres before every ballad. I don't know if we'd missed the up-tempo numbers, but as midnight approached, Pres, his eyes closed, played one aching, gorgeous ballad after another.

"Ladies and gentlemen," said Jo at one point. "One of the finest Basie singers is here tonight. May we convince Miss Avery Hall to join us for a song?"

The applause was polite. Karl was smiling. "Please, let me hear you sing." Pres was snapping his fingers as if he were impatient to begin, so I stood up. The stage was only a few inches above the floor. "*Ghost of a Chance*, Lady Ave," said Pres, closing his eyes. The pianist played the introduction and we were off.

Maybe you've heard those glorious Billie Holiday/Lester

Young records in which Pres' tenor softly wraps itself around Billie's vocals like a silky scarf on a raw winter's day. Well, that's what that magnificent musician—that poet of the saxophone—did for my vocals that night. All the customers in the club were hushed, dreaming along with the song, nodding their heads as if recalling a lost love—which, perhaps, they were. When I looked down, Karl was gazing at me with such love in his blue eyes that I almost cried—but I didn't. I wish that performance had been recorded. With a final cymbal swish from Jo, it was over all too soon.

Back at our table, I felt a tap on my shoulder. "Hold my coat, could you?" asked Buck, trumpet in hand, his dimples flashing. Climbing on stage, he proceeded to play the blues with such subtle power that even Pres was impressed. I looked over at Karl—he was open-mouthed, amazed at the artistry of his new friend.

"I was always a bit of an opera snob," he whispered, leaning over. "But this music has its own power, its own beauty."

I gave him a look that probably said, *You're just figuring this out?*

When the club closed at two a.m., Buck and Jo suggested a nearby all-night bar. Pres, though, floated off into the night. "Night, ladies. And I'm digging *you*, Prince Hubby," he called, his pork-pie hat tilted back, his saxophone case in hand, disappearing down 52nd Street.

"I wonder where he goes," said Jo.

"Man, Pres has ladies all over town, you know that," said Buck. "Come *on*, it's cold."

Soon we were all seated in a warm booth in an empty Ninth Avenue bar. Ella Fitzgerald and Louis Armstrong were singing about that Frim Fram Sauce on the jukebox.

"Just when I think I'm getting somewhere on this horn," said

Buck, sipping his beer, "I listen to Pops and realize how much I still have to learn."

"He's the source, man," said Jo, sipping his own brew.

Karl seemed overcome. "This music of yours," he said, "it's just so. . . ."

"Magnificent?" said Jo.

"Sublime?" said Buck.

"All of it," said Karl. "If I had known that you were playing in Shanghai, I would have been there every evening."

"Thanks, man," said Buck, "but when were you there?"

"From July 1939 until five months ago."

"Ah, I was there in '34 and '35. I was gone by early '36. My band was called the Harlem Gentlemen. We played in the French district in a joint called the Canidrome. Man, some nights Madame Chiang Kai-Shek and her hot little sister would come hear me play. Would you believe that Little Sis took a shine to me?" Looking at Buck, I could believe it. With his cool cat eyes and knowing half-smile, he was the word *handsome* in the flesh.

"Any luck?" asked Jo.

"Man, a gentlemen never tells. . . ."

"Yeah," said Jo with a cackle, "except after Avery's gone home!"

Even Karl joined in with the laughter.

"Hey, Karl," asked Buck. "Did you ever get hit with any prejudice in Shanghai?"

"No—we Jews were pretty much left alone. Even the Japanese let us be. You?"

Buck stared into his half-empty beer, his dimples nowhere in sight. "Wish I could say the same. Now the *Chinese*—man, they treated me like I was an elite. They treated me like an *artist*, man. But it was those others. . . ."

"The Japanese?" asked Jo.

"No, no—I left before they took over. No, it was my own fellow Americans of the, um, *lighter persuasion* who bugged me. So many nights I'd be walking back to the hotel, keeping an eye peeled for the U.S. Marines who wanted to kick my black ass. Couple of times they succeeded too."

Poor Karl looked stricken. "In Germany I never knew this. I thought of your country as the land of the free—"

"Yeah—and the home of the brave," cut in Buck. "Oh, yeah, baby—they were brave alright—especially when it was five Marines against one skinny trumpet player. One night I was walking home a real fine white chick named Betty—she was a dancer at the club—when we was waylaid by five Marines with bricks." Buck shuddered at the memory. "They missed Betty—but look here." He parted his hair. "See that scar? A brick opened up my skull. Took eighteen stitches to close it."

Jo had been quiet—quite unusual for him. "If there's a God, he or she or it should have made us all blind as moles, then this crazy nonsense over what you look like would never have started."

"Amen, Brother Jones," said Buck, "but only one problem with that."

"Yes, Brother Buck?"

"If we were all blind we wouldn't be able to appreciate how hot and *fine* this waitress looks right now."

Our waitress—not aware that she was the topic of a deep theological discussion—delivered a honey-glazed plate of fried chicken. We all dug in.

"Remember those Honey Wagons, Karl?" asked Buck.

I thought my Karl was going to choke. "Oh, my word! Do I ever! Avery, after the factory, I lived in a one-room apartment—about the size of our bedroom's closet. My toilet was a bucket in the corner. Every morning a man driving a wagon would go through the streets, calling—"

"*Moon Dong Lee!*" cut in Buck. "*Moon Dong Lee!*"

"That's exactly what it sounded like," said Karl. "*Moon Dong Lee*!"

"What does it mean?" I asked.

"*Bring out yer poop*," said Buck.

"Yes, indeed," said Karl. "So I would open my one window—first looking up to see if my neighbor above was emptying *his* bucket."

"Man, that could ruin your day," said Buck.

"Indeed," agreed Jo.

"And then the wagon—I won't go into any descriptive details, Ave—would continue down the street," said Buck.

"With the driver calling *Moon Dong Lee*!" said Karl.

I was glad to see that my old friends liked my Karl, and vice versa. Before we knew it, it was close to 3:30 in the morning. Strangely, Buck and Jo had no trouble finding an uptown cab, which left Karl and I on the street, waiting for a downtown ride.

"Let's walk a bit," he suggested. "Maybe we'll see a cab."

Everything was closed, dark. Walking arm in arm, we were quiet. No cabs drove past.

I heard them before I saw them—loud, cackling laughter. There were three of them—all weaving, drunk—and they were headed our way. One had a baseball bat. *Who plays baseball in December?* I remember stupidly thinking.

"Let's cross the street," said Karl in a tight, tense voice.

But it was too late—we were surrounded. Even in the cold night air, I could smell the booze on their breaths. "Are you a nigger lover?" the one with the baseball bat asked. All three laughed as if they had foreseen our future—and it involved a great deal of pain.

"We're not bothering you," said Karl in his precisely accented English. "Please, leave us be."

"Woah—he's a Nazi *and* a nigger lover!" said another.

"I'm not—" Karl began—but before he could finish, the bat had been brought down on his head. I remember screaming—then pain—then nothing.

I woke up in St. Luke's Hospital many hours later with a headache I cannot describe.

"Where's Karl?" I asked the nurse at my bedside.

"*Shh*, honey, you just rest," she said. Feeling a needle sliding into my arm, I dove back into a black sleep.

When I woke up again, a different nurse stood at my bedside, checking a chart. "Doctor?" she called. My eyelids were pulled back and a light shone in my eyes.

"Where's my husband?" I asked.

"He's in the next room, resting," said the doctor, a large man with a wine-colored birthmark on his chin. "There's someone here who wants to say a quick hello."

A chubby, red-faced policeman walked shyly into my room.

"Am I being arrested?" I asked.

The doctor chuckled. "No—this is the man who saved you. The creeps who attacked you are in jail right now."

"My name's Charlie O'Brien," said the policeman. "I own all of your records, Miss Hall. It's an honor."

"You rescued us?"

"I was a block away when I heard you scream. The one with the baseball bat had his leg broken by my billy club. The rest scattered, but we nabbed them."

Trying to hold out my hand, I said a simple, "Thank you, sir."

"I didn't fight in the Battle of the Bulge to return to a country filled with bigotry." Charlie O'Brien was tearing up. "I thought we fought the Nazis *because* they were bigots."

"Where's my husband?"

"That's enough," I heard the doctor say. Another needle slid into my arm and I was gone.

Karl was alive but in a coma, I was told when I again awoke. "You were lucky," said a nurse. "You received a glancing blow. Your husband took a full hit."

"Will he live?" I asked.

"Yes," she said, "but we don't know the extent of the damage to his brain."

I'd suffered a concussion, but Karl had his skull cracked. "I wouldn't look at him just yet," said the nurse.

"And the baby?" I asked.

"You're pregnant?" She rushed to the door. "Doctor!"

The next few days swam by in a series of naps and disjointed awakenings. People visited—Basie, Pres, Jo, Buck, Jimmy, even a cursing Lady Day—and they all seemed to have tears in their eyes at the sight of me. I'd asked several times to see Karl but each time a nurse would tell me, "No, no, it's not time yet." I was told, however, that the baby was fine.

Then one evening a nurse whispered, "Avery, here's a visitor."

A beautiful lady in a mink coat, her warm eyes shining, looked down at me. "Ella!" I said.

"*Shh*, don't sit up," said Ella Fitzgerald. "Here, I'll sit down." Moving a chair close to the bed, she held my hand. I hadn't seen her since that long ago night in the Savoy, but she treated me like a dear friend.

"Listen—next month I'm going to Europe for several months," she said in a lovely voice not all that removed from her singing voice. "I own a big house in the Hollywood Hills, away from everything. There's an orange tree in the backyard *and* a pool *and* a tennis court. Please, when you and your husband are feeling up to it, fly out and stay. Stay as long as you like."

I began to cry. Ella's kindness overwhelmed me.

"You barely know me," I said. "Why are you being so nice?"

Taking one of my hands in both of hers, Ella smiled her glorious smile. "Hey, we're singing sisters. We have to stick together. Besides, we both know what it's like to ride a bus with a bunch of smelly guys."

"They do smell, don't they?"

"Like cattle," she said with a chuckle. "And don't forget how they want you to cook and sew for them, too."

"I never did."

Ella winked. "Me neither."

For a while we were both quiet.

"I hate white people," I said.

Ella looked shocked. "But the man who saved you was a white man."

Of course, I knew she was right, but I said it again: "I hate them."

"Even your husband?"

She had me there—but the needle the nurse jabbed into my arm had me even more, and when I awoke Ella was gone, replaced by Big Joe, the owner of the diner where I had worked all those years before.

"Am I dreaming?" I asked. It had been night when Ella had visited—*if* she had really been there—but now the sun was shining outside the windows.

Joe chuckled. "If you are, couldn't you have dreamed up a better looking specimen than me?"

I held out my arms to be hugged, but he backed off. "No, girl, the doctor said not to shake the bed. How you feeling?" Joe looked the same, only gray.

"They're not telling me how my husband is. I'm worried." My eyes suddenly began to throb.

"I'm sorry, I don't know about that—but, girl, you're looking better than I expected." He suddenly whistled. "Look at this! *Get swinging soon. Love, Ella.* Girl, Ella Fitzgerald done left you flowers!"

"Ha, I thought I dreamt it. Why aren't you at the diner, Joe?"

"Oh, I sold that thing years ago. Got a fair price, too. No, my wife and I just relax and take care of the grandkids."

It hurt to keep my eyes open. "How's Mrs. Wing?"

What's wrong with my eyes? I thought.

"Didn't you hear? Her husband bought a winning lottery ticket about five years ago and they moved to San Francisco. Great lady—I miss her. Just like me, she was very proud of you."

And that's all I remember of Joe's visit.

When I woke up next, an entire week had passed. I was in a new dressing gown and my head was tightly bandaged. The nurse beside my bed called for the doctor, who felt my pulse.

"What happened?" I asked.

The doctor looked into my eyes. "A drifting piece of skull almost cut into your brain. You're lucky to be alive. Raise your left hand for me."

"How's my husband?"

"Raise your right hand. He's getting better every day. For some reason we can't figure, he can't talk, but he understands everything we say to him. He's concerned about you."

The doctor grew blurry behind a film of tears. "Is he going to live?"

"Can your eyes follow this light? Yes, you both are. You can see him tomorrow. But. . . ." And he held both my hands. "I'm very, very sorry, Miss Hall, but you lost the baby."

So my baby was not to be.

"You'll have plenty of other children," the doctor said. I kept my mouth shut.

The next day I was pushed in a wheelchair to Karl's room, which he shared with several others. (I later discovered that Count Basie had paid for my private room). The dear man's head was still bandaged—he looked like an egg. Due to bruising, most of his face was either purple or green. Yet his gentle blue eyes lit up when he saw me, and he held out a hand.

"I love you," I said.

Karl's mouth moved and his eyes looked frustrated. "*Shh*, baby," I said. "The doctor told me that you can't talk—yet. But you will. Just relax."

As we held hands, I told him the news. "Ella Fitzgerald—she's a very famous singer if you don't know—came to see me. While she's off to Europe she's offered us her home in Los Angeles. She says there's a pool. Maybe getting away is just the thing we need."

Karl listened, but he could not talk that day, nor the next, nor the next.

I was half-asleep in my room when Ella returned. Sitting, she took off her gloves. "Man, it's ten degrees outside today. Here—" She handed me an envelope. "The doctor said that you two shouldn't fly—something about your head injuries and pressure. So here are two train tickets—to be used whenever—and the front door key to my house. I wrote down the address on the front of the envelope. I won't be back until June, so use the house as long as you wish—even when I get back. There's plenty of room for all of us."

"How can I thank you?" I said.

Laughing, Ella said, "You just did."

We talked about this and that—mostly music—for a spell,

and then she left, leaving behind the scent of lilacs.

Two months later, on a drizzly Tuesday, Karl and I boarded a train at Pennsylvania Station, bound for California. Basie was there to see us off.

"Don't you be talking Karl's ear off—you hear me, girl?" he said. "You let me know if she's her usual difficult self, okay, Karl?"

Karl nodded—something he hadn't been able to do even the week before.

"I'm bringing a small quartet out to the coast in August. I'll give you a call," said Basie. "Take care, you two. Soak up some of that California sunshine."

And we were off.

Twenty-One

We had our own compartment, with a sitting room and a double berth. Karl spent most of the trip gazing out the window. I had no idea what my husband was thinking—but I certainly know what *I* was thinking: *If this good man had never met me, he would never have been attacked. He would never have been out that night, he would not have been seen walking with a black woman. He would now be fine. He would be able to talk.* The trip took four days and although I did enjoy the scenery—particularly when the train climbed through the snow-capped Rocky Mountains—for most of the trip I roasted myself alive. At times when I looked in his eyes, it was Karl—he was there, communicating, just not with speech. However, at other times his blue eyes were galaxies away, lost somewhere remote and chilly. And I spent so much time taking care of my husband that I never had a chance to mourn our baby.

Before we'd left the hospital, the doctor had spoken to me: "Your husband's x-rays show minor brain damage—but this type usually repairs itself. Yet I emphasize the word *usually*. Your husband could begin speaking tomorrow, next year—or never. There's so much about the brain that is still a mystery."

I hadn't been in California since a Basie tour in the early 40s.

When a taxi brought us up into the Hollywood Hills, stopping in front of a rambling ranch house with two palm trees in the yard, it was all so lovely I couldn't believe my eyes—or our luck.

"This is it, Karl," I said. The driver helped us with our luggage.

Ella's living room, three walls of glass, looked out on a lush green lawn with a pool in the middle and a tennis court beyond. As promised, an orange tree, filled with fruit, bloomed in the center. A fence at yard's end blocked off an almost sheer cliff, with the City of Angels below.

"Want to take a swim?" I asked.

Karl shook his head *No*, wandering off to take a nap. Ella's bedroom was easy to spot, with a bed as big as Rhode Island, but the two guest rooms were almost as fine. For dinner I cooked up two mushroom omelettes, but Karl slept on. After living through the coldest New York City winter in years, I found the evening balmy, and I sat alone on a lounge in the backyard, sipping a glass of wine, enjoying the twinkling lights of 1948 Los Angeles being switched on far below.

During the first week Karl mostly slept. The doctor had told me that he would still need his rest—his skull *had* been cracked—but I missed him. I wasn't lonely, though, because Ella's gardener, a black gentleman named Henry, dropped by every day to water the plants and flowers and tend to the pool.

"So you married yourself a white man," he said one evening just before he left. The tone was not nasty.

"Yes, I did. Karl is Jewish, from Germany."

"Did he being white and you being black have anything to do with the state of his head?"

Briefly, I told him the story. "That's a shame, a crying shame," he said, wiping his forehead with a green handkerchief. "Years ago my mama suffered a head injury—caused by a fall—and she just wasn't herself. The doctor told me to read to her, so I did, regularly."

"Did it help?" It seemed like the man I'd married had sailed off to a foreign land.

"Seemed to. Before I knew it she was her old self, bossing me around." He smiled. "Now I don't know if the reading brought her back, but it was a nice way to spend the time."

"Thank you, Henry."

The next morning I walked down the hill to a shopping plaza. I opened a checking account, bought a gallon of milk, and stepped into a small bookstore. After browsing, I found something interesting: *Swing That Music*, by Louis Armstrong. I didn't know Pops, but so many of my friends did, and had told me stories about him, that I felt like I'd known him for years. So every afternoon I insisted that Karl sit in the sun by the pool while I read to him about Louis Armstrong's childhood in New Orleans.

"I was in New Orleans back when I sang with Basie," I said. Karl's blue eyes were studying the sky. "One morning I was sitting on a bench by the Mississippi when an old man strolled up. . . ." As I told the story, Karl began to look at me and for the first time in many weeks he seemed to be truly listening. It was a bit clumsy, but he insisted on holding my hand while I read Louis' book to him.

The weeks passed by in a blur of sunshine and swimming and oranges and books. I cooked simple but nourishing meals, I read to Karl every afternoon, and often in the evenings Henry and his wife Carol, a gorgeous gal, would drop by for wine and conversation.

"Avery told me about some of your experiences in Dachau," said Henry one evening. We were seated by Ella's pool. The warm breeze smelled of flowers. Karl nodded, the first time in weeks. "I fought against the Nazis," continued Henry. "I was mostly in Italy. Saw combat five times. I try not to think too hard about it, but I know that I killed men."

"Some nights he thrashes and shouts in his sleep," said Carol.

"But when I read about what the Nazis did to the good Jewish people . . . well, it makes me feel that maybe I'll be forgiven."

Reaching over, Karl placed his hand on Henry's and kept it there. His lips moved and his eyes searched Henry's. It was obvious that he wanted to say something—to thank him, perhaps—but he simply couldn't. His frustration was painful to see.

"Don't worry—I know what you're saying, Brother Karl," said Henry.

One bright California morning, I could've sworn I heard the Basie Whistle—*I want you to get way back, babe*—followed by Ella's doorbell ringing. When I opened the door, there stood Papa Jo Jones, dressed in white tennis shorts, with a buxom blonde, also in white, on his arm. Not surprisingly, the smell of Wrigley's Spearmint was in the air.

"Ella told me that I have free use of her tennis court," he said, wrapping me in a bear hug. "This is Lana. Lana, this is Avery."

Refusing any breakfast, they dove onto that court and played tennis for the next two hours—and let me tell you, Jo and that babe could *play.* Lana was bouncing all over the place, huffing and puffing, but I don't think Jo minded one bit.

Afterwards, we sat under the orange tree, sipping orange juice while Lana took a swim. I thought that maybe I should wake Karl up—he would've enjoyed seeing Lana in the pool—but I decided to let him sleep.

"Nice lady friend," I said.

"Actually, I *don't* want her to get way back," said Jo with a chuckle.

"Yeah, I bet."

"It must've been terrifying, Ave," said Jo. My unique friend looked close to tears. Despite the sudden shift, I knew what he meant.

"I try not to think about it."

"Worse than Memphis?"

I winced—but then thought about it. "Yeah, it was. And you know why? Because in Memphis I was only worried about myself. In New York I was terrified for my husband, too. It made it worse."

Jo sipped his juice. "Makes sense."

Before they left, Jo cupped my face in his warm hands. "You're one of my kiddies, kid. If you ever need Papa Jo, you know I'll be there."

"I know, Jo. Thanks."

And the finest drummer in all of jazz, in his tennis whites, strolled off with a Hollywood blonde, resplendent in a yellow dress, on his arm.

Back in New York, our mail was gathered up every two weeks by our landlord, packed in a cardboard box, and mailed to us. (When I handed him a large check to cover several months' rent, I had included extra money for postage.) One morning in April the latest box included a light green envelope postmarked *Berlin.* Karl was sitting beneath the orange tree, looking up at the sky, but his eyes poured into mine when I asked, "Can I open it?"

The entire letter, not surprisingly, was written in German, with the word *Beschluss* printed at the top in bold letters. Grabbing it, Karl seemed to devour the words. Then sighing, he devoured them again. For at least ten long minutes he sat, his eyes closed. It was a cloudless California morning, with the smell of Ella's orange tree and the sound of the birds.

"My father is long dead," said Karl, his eyes still closed.

I didn't know whether to burst into tears at the news—or leap up in joy at the sound of my husband's voice.

"I'm so sorry," I said.

Opening his eyes, he smiled, but beyond sadly. "Why—because you have to listen to my annoying voice again?"

What happened next is private.

"*Beschluss* means *Decision,*" said Karl much later. We were back outside, sitting in Ella's lawn chairs. "Here's all my father's information: *Heinz George Flach*—he went by *George. Born in Posen on 22 September 1880.* He was 31 when I was born. I didn't know that. Look here: *Berlin-Schoneberg*—that was our district—*Meranerstrasse 11*—that was our street address." His finger pointed. "It says my father was taken by the *East Transport* in March 1943 to . . ." He swallowed hard. ". . . Auschwitz. That was the very worst of Hitler's camps—in Poland. I'm quoting: '*Because of extreme age, he is assumed not to have lived much longer.*' It only says he was dead by 31 December 1943. '*Do not come to Auschwitz expecting a cemetery. Your father's body was burned in an oven.*' And look: '*There is no charge for this information.*' Typical German."

Karl was quiet for so long that I feared he had once again slipped into muteness. But then he gently touched my face. "Thank you, my Avery, for taking such good care of me. Don't worry. I'm fine. It's a relief to now know. I knew he was dead, but not knowing *how* was the torture. Perhaps he died quickly." He burst into tears. "I can still see him on that train platform, waving goodbye. . . ."

Not knowing what to say, I said nothing.

I simply held my husband for a long, long time.

Twenty-Two

The next month was the honeymoon we had never enjoyed. My Karl was back.

"What were you thinking when you couldn't talk?" I asked one morning. We had already swam in Ella's pool before breakfast. Henry was trimming the hedges on the edge of the property.

"At times it was frustrating—I knew what I wanted to say to you, but could not. At other times it felt like a dream. I recall almost nothing of the train trip—except one thing. I woke up one night and you were sleeping. I must have watched your beautiful face for over an hour. I was thinking how lucky I was to meet you."

The guilt had not gone away. "Meeting me was the reason why you were beaten."

"Ha! You call that a beating?" Gently, he tapped his skull. "Once you've been beaten by Nazis, my dear, you can take anything."

"I don't know if I want to go back to New York," I said. "It could happen again."

He took both my hands in his. "It could happen here, too. It could happen anywhere. We just have to keep our wits."

May and most of June flew by. With Henry's help, we rented a car and took drives along the Pacific Coast Highway. A good-sized royalty check for *Avery's Blues* arrived one morning and we decided to cash it and drive to Monterey. We rented a cabin by the Pacific Ocean and simply enjoyed being together. I believe it was in Monterey that we conceived—and this time we did not lose the baby.

One morning in late June, back at Ella's house, we heard a key turning in the front door lock. "Hello? Don't be frightened," said that familiar, girlish voice. "It's just me—back from Europe."

Ella was home.

That night she cooked up a feast for us—salmon and steaks on the grill with three types of salads. "I hope you don't mind, but I invited a friend over. He should be here soon."

We were in the backyard, watching Ella grill, when the doorbell rang. "Could you get that, Avery?" asked Ella. "I don't want the meat to burn."

Opening the door, I saw that snaggle-toothed grin, that porkpie hat, that long coat (even in the California heat). There stood Pres, holding a paper bag.

"Big eyes for you, Lady Ave!" he said, hugging me, lifting me off my feet. As always, Pres smelled of witch hazel and a fresh shave.

"Lady Fitz! Prince Hubby!" he said in the backyard, wrapping them both in a warm hug. "Here, I brought some fine-as-wine wine, because we both *know* that Lady Ella can *burn. Mmm!*"

Soon Henry and Carol joined us, and we enjoyed a marvelous meal in Ella's backyard. She clearly enjoyed cooking for her guests and couldn't do enough for us. "Last year she bought us a home," said Henry when our hostess left for the kitchen.

"We'd been living in a dumpy apartment," said Carol. "One day Ella said, 'I have a surprise for you. Let's go for a drive.' She took us to this beautiful bungalow, handed us the keys and said, 'Here's your new home.'"

"Are you telling that silly bungalow story again, Carol?" said Ella, emerging from the house with a key-lime pie.

"Yes—and I'll tell it 'til the day I die," said Carol, embracing a clearly embarrassed Ella.

Naturally, Pres had to whip out a small glass bottle of witch hazel with cotton balls, and we all had to partake. The rest of the evening passed with Pres telling tales both tall and true. One story about a lady wrestler in Paris made us gasp with laughter.

"You know," said Ella to Karl and me, "you two should think of moving to Paris."

"Bells," said Pres. "Pres has big eyes for gay Par-ee. Few cats seem hung up on skin tone there. Old Pres is treated like a great artist by the French ladies."

"You *are* a great artist," I said.

Standing, Pres bowed low. "Smotherin' heights, Lady Ave. Have you ever been to the City of Lights, Prince Hubby?"

"No, but my parents honeymooned there," said Karl. "They always spoke of seeing Toulouse Lautrec in a dance-hall, sketching away."

Ella smiled. "Something to keep in mind. You're always going to receive looks and comments in this country. Why not move to a city that will leave you alone?"

Pres beamed. *"Madame Fitz, mes yeux sont grandes pour cette idee."*

So feel free to picture the three of us—Karl, baby George, and me—in an airy apartment on the Left Bank, taking long walks with a stroller through the narrow, cobble-stoned streets, buying bread from our local *patisserie*.

Picture us being left blessedly in peace.

Picture Karl finding a job as an accountant at a bank on the *rue de Rivoli*.

Picture our apartment, the scene of parties filled with music and laughter and poignant memories when Basie and Pres and Ella and Buck and Little Jimmy and Papa Jo play Paris.

Picture me singing one night a week at a basement club called the *Blue Note*—many times with a visiting Pres sitting in—and recording the occasional song for a small French record label.

Picture my thick head, now flecked with the occasional gray hair, finally learning how to speak fluent French.

Picture George growing up to be a spirited, opinionated, honorable young man—with his mother's brown skin and his father's blue eyes.

Picture a beautiful, spirited daughter-in-law—and more-than-beautiful grandbabies.

Picture Karl and I realizing as the years pass that we did not make a mistake by falling in love.

Picture an elderly couple, holding hands, strolling by the Seine.

Because all of that is exactly what happened.

The Musicians Accompanying Our Girl Singer

William "Count" Basie (1904-1984): Born in Red Bank, New Jersey, Bill Basie headed west to Kansas City to lead one of the swingingest bands in musical history. Whether leading his *Old Testament Band* of the 1930s or his *New Testament Band* of the 50s/60s/70s/80s, Count Basie could "swing a band with one finger." Says the Count himself: "I just think *swing* is a matter of some good things put together that you can really pat your foot by."

Lester "Pres" Young (1909-1959): The lonely poet of the tenor saxophone, Pres started his own school of playing—an airy, dancing, light-but-always-swinging style that captivated dozens of disciples. With his porkpie hat and crepe soled shoes, Pres was the epitome of hip, speaking his own jargon. Many linguists feel that it was Lester who coined the terms *hip, cool*, and nicknamed New York City *The Big Apple*. The recordings he made with The Count Basie Orchestra and with his dear friend Billie Holiday are American music at its finest.

Papa Jo Jones (1911-1985): One of jazz's top drummers—the "man who played like the wind"—Jo was also one of the music's defining characters. An autodidact, Jones loved to lecture his "kiddies" on the verities of Jazz: "Jazz is the most spiritual of all musics," he told Dan Morgenstern, "a delicate thing. You can't play it unless you have found yourself, and it takes time to find ourselves." Whether he was playing tennis, reading four books at once, or smiling as he stoked the engines of the Count Basie Orchestra, Jo Jones was artistry in motion.

Billie "Lady Day" Holiday (1915-1959): One of the two very greatest singers of Jazz, Billie thought of her voice as another instrument in the band. According to Richard Cook: "(Billie's) behind-the-beat delivery and the supple elegance of her phrasing have the individual grace and strength of a singular jazz musician." Although drink, drugs, and heartless lovers led to a tragic early death, those who knew her, like Nat Hentoff, remember a "funny, salty, generous woman—and what a skilled mimic!" Bring Billie's music into your life and you will never stop listening.

Ella Fitzgerald (1917-1996): One of the two very greatest singers of Jazz, Ella never forgot her humble beginnings, stunning people with her generosity. With her girlishly light voice, she led the Chick Webb Band after its leader's death, soldiering on with a grit that showed her strength. In later years she recorded the immortal monument to the Great American Songbook: *The Ella Fitzgerald Songbooks* (Verve Records). Any dreary day can be brightened with Ella.

Walter "Big 'Un" Page (1900-1957): The bassist of the "All-American Rhythm Section," Page first led his own band, the legendary *Walter Page's Blue Devils*, gathering Lester Young and Count Basie under his wing. The Blue Devils only made one record, in 1929, and Big 'Un soon joined the band of his rival, Bennie Moten. After Moten's death in 1935, the band morphed into the Count Basie Orchestra. Page was the rock-solid yet swinging anchor of the band.

Freddie Green (1911-1987): Joining Basie in 1937, Freddie stayed, with only one brief interruption, until the leader's death in 1984. His unobtrusive rhythm guitar playing gave the band its smooth engine-like swing. "You should never hear the guitar by itself," Freddie once said. "It should be part of the drums so it sounds like the drummer is playing chords."

Buck Clayton (1911-1991): In 1936 when Buck brought his drenched-in-blues trumpet to Basie, he had already played all over the country—even leading his own band in Shanghai, China. "Buck was the most beautiful man I ever laid eyes on," said Lady Day. Whether on mute or open horn, Buck brought soul and artistry to every song.

Herschel Evans (1909-1939): A month shy of 30 when he died, Herschel was "the greatest jazz musician I ever played with in my life," according to Papa Jo Jones. With his deep Texas tone, his tenor saxophone was the perfect compliment to Lester Young's lighter, floating solos. The public believed Herschel and Pres to be rivals, but they were brothers, and Pres was never quite the same after Evans' death.

Harry "Sweets" Edison (1915-1999): Pres gave Harry his nickname and it was apropos: With his spare, bluesy, not-wasting-a-note sound, Sweets Edison was also Frank Sinatra's favorite trumpeter. Along with the tougher sounding Buck Clayton, Sweets gave Basie a broad trumpet palette from which to draw.

"Little" Jimmy Rushing (1902-1972): Writer Ralph Ellison writes of lying in bed at night as a boy in Oklahoma City, hearing *Mr. Five By Five*'s voice in the summer air, singing from nearby ballrooms. Like Basie, Jimmy was a Blue Devil before joining Bennie Moten's band, which became the Count Basie Orchestra. On songs like "I Left My Baby," "Goin' to Chicago," and "Good Morning Blues," Rushing brought his profound bluesy soul to Swing .

Dickie Wells (1907-1985): Before joining Basie in 1938, Dickie had already recorded one of the great trombone records, "Dickie Wells' Blues," in Paris. During his dozen years with the band, Wells gave unique humor and spirit to the Count Basie Orchestra.

Buddy Tate (1912-2001): Buddy—another Texas tenorman—had the unenviable task of replacing Herschel Evans in the Count Basie Orchestra, but he did, with style, grace, and his own swinging sound.

The Author

Portrait by Hannah Carlon

Mick Carlon is well into his third decade as a public school English teacher at both the high and middle school levels. When not grading papers, he can be found driving his wife, Lisa, and daughters, Hannah and Sarah, crazy with his incessant playing of jazz CDs. "Jazz musicians are among America's most fearless artists, and if young people will only give the music of artists such as Louis Armstrong, Count Basie, Duke Ellington, Ella Fitzgerald, Billie Holiday and Lester Young a try, they will make enriching friends for life." Mick's first children's novel, *Riding on Duke's Train*, is about a boy's adventures traveling with Duke Ellington and His Famous Orchestra. His second novel, *Travels With Louis*, deals with a young man's adventures with his surrogate grandfather, Louis Armstrong.

About the Photographer

Heinz Praeger (1911-1997) was born and raised in Berlin, Germany. After experiencing *Kristallnacht* in the German town of Kitzingen, he was shipped to Dachau. Able to escape the Nazis' first concentration camp, Heinz fled to Shanghai, China, where he lived from 1939 to 1947. In Shanghai, according to Heinz, "my hobby, photography, became my profession." Heinz's photographs are now part of the permanent collection at the United States Holocaust Memorial Museum in Washington, D.C.

Links

Visit Leapfrog Press on Facebook
Google: Facebook Leapfrog Press

or enter

https://www.facebook.com/pages/Leapfrog-Press/222784181103418

Leapfrog Press Website
www.leapfrogpress.com

Author Website
www.mickcarlon.com

About the Type

This book was set in Adobe Caslon, a typeface originally released by William Caslon in 1722. His types became popular throughout Europe and the American colonies, and printer Benjamin Franklin used hardly any other typeface. The first printings of the American Declaration of Independence and the Constitution were set in Caslon. .

Designed by John Taylor-Convery
Composed at JTC Imagineering, Santa Maria, CA